Born To Be Badass

(Book 3 of the Demon Employment series)

Born To Be Wicked – Book 1
Born To Be Devilish – Book 2
Born To Be Badass – Book 3

Shade Owens
www.shadeowens.com

Edited by Nikki Busch
www.nikkibuschediting.com

RED RAVEN PUBLISHING

WARNING: this story contains a lot of swearing (many f-bombs), violence, and sexual content.

Intended for readers 18+

Prologue

He stares into me, his blazing blue eyes resembling shards of glass. When I don't look away, he pushes the tip of his medieval sword into my throat. His grip tightens and his forearm muscles harden. "You have some nerve showing up here, Alexis."

Rapid footsteps echo behind me, but they stop the moment my attacker's eyes roll up.

Lowering his head, he glares at Ace and Drax and a villainous smile stretches his face. "One more step and your little friend here loses her head."

This can't be happening.

It isn't possible.

"What's the matter, Alexis? Were you expecting someone else?"

"Yeah, actually."

He pushes his sword forward again and I wince. In any other scenario, no way would I be so complacent with a man threatening my life, but right now, I'm too taken aback to think clearly. If he's still standing after what happened, what else is he capable of?

Through the room's massive window, the golden sun disappears behind San Halos's tallest towers, filling the room with dreary darkness. His face, now shaded and seemingly featureless, moves closer to me. Although I can barely see him now, I hear him smile—a wet clicking sound that has me picturing that striking face of his. "This is the last place I expected to find you, Alexis, but now that you're here, let's have some fun, shall we?"

CHAPTER 1

For a moment, I wonder if maybe I've walked into the wrong apartment.

Rachel warned me there was a lot of damage after she accidentally summoned a griffin, but I didn't expect *this*. Both Ace and Drax stand behind me with arms crossed over their chests and their lips as tight as fresh wounds bound together by a dozen stitches.

I mean, it shouldn't bother me, right? It's not like I own this place. Besides, it wasn't eye candy to begin with. But as I trace the massive claw marks across my living room—three-inch grooves cutting straight through my parquet floor—I can't help but feel a bit bummed.

My couch, old as hell itself, is split into two as if someone took a giant pair of scissors and snipped right down its middle. On the left piece is a pile of wiry white hair—Mr. Mushroom's hair. Poor little guy. He's going to be distraught when I tell him his favorite couch is done for.

Sighing, I walk over big chunks of drywall and

debris, and make my way into my bedroom.

"Where's she going?" Ace whispers behind me.

Drax says something about *supplies*, and he's right.

I blast my closet door open and start throwing piles of clothes out until I see the latch—something even Drax doesn't know about. Using my thumb claw, I break apart the lock and open my poorly designed secret compartment. It's a hole I punched through the floor that I later covered with a few pieces of plywood and two sturdy latches.

It may not be perfect, but hey, it's not like anyone would ever suspect anything unusual about a woman's pile of laundry. I reach inside the hole, grimacing as spiderwebs tickle the back of my hand, and extract a sturdy plastic bin you'd use to store construction tools.

The closet's dim overhead light reflects off my weapons as I place them next to my shoe collection.

"Everything okay in there?" Ace asks from a safe distance.

See? No one wants to go near a woman's closet.

"All good." As I stare at my two Glocks sitting atop a pile of daggers, grenades, tasers, and brass knuckles, I inhale a deep breath. After I lost Jamal—the young boy I saved and viewed as my own son—I swore I'd never use guns again. He told me many times how much he hated guns being that he came from a rundown neighborhood where gunshots went off almost every night. But I never listened to him. All I did was assure him that these were for our protection. It was only after he died that I honored his wish and stuck to bulletless weapons.

But now we're at war.

I reach inside, pull out the guns, and wipe off a layer of dust coating the cool metal.

Man, I missed these things. While I may be good with a crossbow, or any other weapon for that matter, I'm one hell of a shot when it comes to guns.

Smirking, I push aside a handful of wooden stakes and pull out my weapons belt. "Haven't seen you in a while, either," I say. I stand up and clip the belt around my waist before loading it with my Glocks, some stakes, and a few other weapons I've collected throughout my lifetime.

The second I walk back out into the living room, Ace's eyebrow pulls up and Drax's jaw hangs slack. But before they can say anything, I stiffen my back, plant my hands over my belt, and say, "Why're you guys just standing there? We don't have all day. Let's get this show on the road."

CHAPTER 2

"Why isn't she back yet?" I say, pacing across the remains of our motel room.

Ace reaches inside the broken refrigerator and pulls out a water bottle. Calmly, he opens it, takes a sip, and wipes the water bubbles off the dark scruff on his face.

If I weren't so worried about Rachel, I'd throw him through the wall again and have my way with him. He stands there, his round shoulders drawn back with such confidence you'd think he had it all figured out. When he catches me staring, he narrows his eyes on me—a seductive look that makes me wonder if he's using his Incubus Lure on me.

But I'm sure he isn't. We made a pact that neither of us would use our seduction abilities to manipulate the other, and after the stunt he pulled a few hours ago—allowing me to feed off his life force, which almost killed him—I know I can trust this man.

"We knew this was a risk," Drax says, his eyes

inspecting every inch of the motel room as if searching for sprinkles of weed.

Mr. Mushroom jumps up onto my lap and snuggles his face into my side.

I dig my nails into the loose skin of his back. "I'm glad you're safe, buddy." Loving every bit of it, he throws his head back and lets out a raspy howl.

Both Drax and Ace stare at me, likely waiting for me to blurt out some ingenious plan. There's one problem though: I don't have a plan. I banked on Rachel coming back with Zerachu and that together, we'd figure all of this out.

I'm willing to bet no one knows who's behind all of this. Not even the Council of Elders. I think back to Clock Dragon's reaction when I boldly asked him where Lucius was hiding the book. He thought I was messing with him.

Is that why whoever's behind this decided to lock Zerachu up? What better way to cause chaos than to trap the Great Witch? If anyone would know what the hell is going on, it's her. Either that, or she'd know how to fix this, which is a threat to the person orchestrating this mess.

"We should move forward," Ace says, and I clench my teeth.

He must sense my hurt. The moment I make eye contact with him, he bows his head apologetically. "I'm sure Rachel is safe. She might be facing a few challenges, but that girl is a smart witch. She'll make it back to us. Until then, though, we should use the Interruptus spell to our advantage."

Twenty-four hours.

Or at least, that's what Ace thinks our timeframe will be, based on similar spells used in the past.

I turn to Riskus, who watches us silently with no hint of emotion on his face. I'm sure deep down, he's freaking out as much as I am, if not more. Rachel's his master, and if she were here to correct me, she'd say his *friend.*

"Can you hold down the fort again?" I ask him.

He nods like a trained soldier, and Mr. Mushroom's ears fold flat on his head.

"Thanks, Riskus. We'll be back as soon as we can. If Rachel comes back, please keep her here until we get back." I jerk my chin out at him. "And please don't forget to feed Mr. Mushroom."

The little demon nods again.

I shift my focus onto Ace. "Can you take us to the Jamieson Hotel?"

He gives me a look that surely translates to *Are you sure that's where you want to go?*

I'm more than sure. There's one way out of this. We must collaborate with the vampires. Whoever stole the artifacts needs to be stopped before this war gets out of hand, if it isn't already too late, and if there's one place to gather information on the vampires, it's Jamieson's place.

Right when Drax is about to open what appears to be a stale bag of potato chips, I say, "Can you take us there, or not?"

I'm tempted to question Ace about my new demigod abilities and whether I'll be able to harness enough power to teleport the way he does. I mean, if my father gave him that gift, wouldn't it be coursing through my veins, too?

But now isn't the time to fantasize about being able to appear anywhere I want.

"Of course," Ace says, straightening his muscular back. He extends two open palms and waits for Drax and I to grab them. The moment the warmth of his hand touches mine, our eyes lock, and I find myself staring at his juicy lips, his strong jawline, his round shoulders—

I'm about to lick my lips when everything disappears and we stumble into Jamieson's office.

I stick a finger inside my ear and wiggle it to regain my balance. "I have to ask, Ace, how do you teleport to a place you've never seen before?"

For a second, my heart almost climbs up into my throat. What if he *has* seen this place before? What if he's working with Jamieson? What if maybe, all along, I was wrong about Ace? I'm not typically wrong about anyone, but with him, I have my doubts.

Why? Because his sexiness clouds my mind.

I hate how we have such a strong bond. I met the guy a short time ago, yet it feels like I've known him my entire life. Well, I suppose maybe I have. All along, he's been following me. Maybe it isn't his intentions I don't trust—maybe I'm too afraid of caring about him.

Fuck, I hate introspective shit.

He must sense my worry—he rests his large hand on my shoulder and says, "It's an energy thing. It's hard to explain, but I can feed off—"

Suddenly, another voice overtakes his, sending chills up my spine.

"Well, well, well."

I spin around and my wrist blades come flying out of their hidden compartments. With fists clenched and posture hunched, I stand face-to-face with Jamieson.

What the fuck is he doing here? Feebles aren't supposed to be on Earth—not after the Interruptus spell. He can't possibly be fae, can he? We've had plenty of conversations about how much he hates demons and anything magical, and how if he had the choice, he'd burn them all alive.

It's clear his anger comes from a place of hurt. Doesn't take a psychologist to figure that out. But he's never come out and explained to me why he hates them so much, and I haven't questioned it, either. It was more important for me to keep my true identity hidden from him than to try to understand his.

"How—" I try, but nothing comes out.

"What's the matter, Alexis? You look like you've seen a ghost."

This doesn't make any sense. If he were fae, I

would have sensed it. What kind of bullshit is this? Is he a hologram? I mean, I wouldn't put it past him. The guy has more money than every bank in San Halos. Then again, he also owns them all. If he wanted to create an illusion of himself, he'd have no trouble hiring the best of the best.

I flare my nostrils. "What are you doing here, Jamieson?"

He steps slowly toward me, his shiny leather shoes ticking against his spotless office tiles.

I bend my knees, prepared to lunge if I have to. One wrong move on his part and he can kiss his dick goodbye.

"You look confused, Alexis. Is there something you want to tell me?"

Forget his dick. Maybe I'll slice those lips right off his arrogant face and feed it to his fish. Does he know I'm fae? Has he known all along? Has he been playing me this whole time despite his hatred of fae?

But what happens next is all too sudden for me to react. As if by magic, he draws a medieval-looking sword and presses its cold, sharp tip into the base of my throat. What appeared to be amusement on his face transforms into a venomous scowl. "You have some nerve showing up here, Alexis."

Footsteps run toward me, but the moment Jamieson's hateful slits turn on Drax and Ace, my friends stop in their tracks.

He lowers his head and glares at Ace and Drax. "One more step and your little friend here loses her head."

This can't be happening.

It isn't possible.

"What's the matter, Alexis? Were you expecting someone else?"

"Yeah, actually—"

He pushes his sword forward again and I glower at him. In any other scenario, no way would I be so complacent with a man threatening my life, but right now, I'm too taken aback to think clearly.

As the sun sets, filling his office with a dim orange glow, he lowers his head until I'm barely able to make out his features. "This is the last place I expected to find you, Alexis, but now that you're here, let's have some fun, shall we?"

CHAPTER 3

I glare at him, wondering why I didn't slit his throat when I had the chance.

"Sit," Jamieson orders, and with a click of his fingers, I find myself strapped to his office chair.

I tug, but my wrists are bound with what appear to be magical cuffs. The red energy swirls around my arms like melted licorice and extends down to my ankles. There's no way out of this one. Ace hurries forward, prepared to risk his life to protect me, when Jamieson clicks his fingers again and Ace disappears with a loud poof.

In his place is a small black cricket. It twirls in circles, chirps, and jumps up onto one of Jamieson's accent chairs.

A few feet away, Drax's eyes bulge out of his scaly green head and he takes a step back.

"Smart boy," Jamieson says, moving toward the cricket.

"Don't you fucking touch him!" I shout, but Jamieson doesn't slow down.

Without a care in the world, he slaps Ace off his

chair, then raises his shiny shoe and stomps down hard on the cricket.

"You son of a bitch!" I shout, jerking my body from side to side.

The chair hops with me, but the restraints remain as firm as ever.

Smiling, Jamieson twirls his foot as if putting out a cigarette butt, and a hot rage rises inside of me. He killed Ace. He fucking killed him. I swear to the gods, if I get ahold of him, he'll wish for death.

The veins in my temples throb, and my face feels fiery hot. Although I can't see myself, I imagine I'm as red as a ripe tomato.

I'll kill him. I'll fucking kill him.

As the anger spreads through me, I scream as loud as I can and pull my wrists upward. The red flow of magic breaks apart with loud zapping noises, and Jamieson's features instantly invert.

"How—" he begins, then mutters something incomprehensible.

Suddenly, iron cuffs appear out of thin air and wrap themselves around my forearms.

"Breaking through magic," he says. "That's a first."

I want to let out some sarcastic remark, but I can't. Jamieson's right. It is a first, isn't it? I've never heard of anyone being able to manipulate magic with brute physical force. It's not like I'm magical, so how is this possible?

I try to jerk again, but nothing happens. Slowly,

I shift my attention to Jamieson's shoe and my throat begins to swell.

How did I let this happen? Ace.

Jamieson fixes his suit's cuffs and elevates his chin. "Tell me, Alexis, why are you here? You stole from me, disappeared, and now you've returned. For what? To steal from me again?"

"What are you?" I say through gritted teeth.

He's not a demon; of that I'm certain. I would have smelled him. Witches and warlocks, on the other hand, often go undetected because everything about them screams feeble until they perform an act of magic.

He smirks sideways at me. "The better question is, what are *you*?"

At the back of the room, Drax stands, looking awkward and fidgeting with his hands. It's obvious he wants to come to my defense, but he doesn't know what to do. If we were dealing with Jamieson—the man I thought was a feeble—Drax would likely set aside his gentle giant personality and rage out on the man. But Jamieson has magic and we don't.

Although Drax might want to save the day, he knows me well enough to know that I don't want him to attempt anything. I've already lost Ace. I can't lose Drax, too.

Slowly, Jamieson moves toward his Italian leather office chair, rolls it away from his desk, and sets it in front of me. He sits down as if descending into his throne, and with his stubbled chin pointed out, stares at me.

"I hope you know how much your selfishness will cost you, Alexis."

I breathe out hard through flared nostrils. "What the fuck do you want, Jamieson?"

Without hesitating, he says, "For you to suffer."

I can't believe what's coming out of his asshole mouth. So I stole from him on my last job. Big whoop. He's acting like I killed his entire fucking family. The dude's filthy rich. No way did my theft of a few million dollars affect him so badly. Besides, he was a dick about it. He should have never asked me to grab Veerka's necklace when that wasn't part of the original deal.

"What's this about, Jamieson? Because it sure as hell isn't the bit of money I pocketed. And I doubt it's about the necklace I never brought you."

He leans back, looking amused. "You're a bright one, Alexis. I did always like you."

"You sure about that?" I ask.

Suddenly, his features sharpen demonically and he leans in close. "You were supposed to kill her."

Who is he talking about? Veerka? How does he even know she isn't dead? And then it hits me—Jamieson's in bed with the vampires, which means he's close to Lucius. And if that's the case, he knows Veerka returned.

Oh, yeah. I guess I did fuck him over pretty badly. Not only did I take money for a job I didn't even do, I took more for an item I never brought to him.

"Why do you care so much?" I ask.

He shakes his head, losing his cool. "You fucked with my plans, Alexis." He jabs a stiff finger at my face. "You fucked me big-time."

Clearing his throat, he regains composure and brushes a few loose strands of hair back onto his perfectly gelled blond hair. "You've cost me an empire." He stops, his eyes wandering toward the ceiling. "But I suppose I should be thanking you. Your little stunt brought about another plan. One far greater than my initial one."

"What are you talking about?" I ask.

He throws his head back and laughs maniacally. "You have no idea, do you?"

I glower at him.

"We're at war, Alexis."

And to think I once found his English accent sexy. Now, all I want to do is materialize his words and shove them down his throat until he chokes on them.

"And soon, San Halos will be mine."

San Halos? What's this guy smoking, and why does he care about this city so much? I mean, I get that San Halos is pretty much the capital of all things fae, but what's he planning?

That's when it hits me. Is Jamieson responsible for the stolen book and talisman?

"You know, it wasn't all that difficult convincing

my son to turn against his mother," he says.

Smugly, he plucks at the cuffs of his suit again and crosses his legs to reveal silky red socks under his black pants. The more I look at him, the more I imagine him to be the spawn of Hades.

"What the fuck are you babbling about?" I snap.

His son? What does his son have to do with the war between the vampires and the rest of the shadow dwellers? And he never told me he had a son. Not that we've ever had in-depth conversations.

"Oh, surely you've met him, Alexis. I believe he's with your friend as we speak. What's her name again? Rachel?"

I lunge forward, prepared to rip his face off with my teeth.

"If you fucking hurt—"

"You have no one other than yourself to blame, Alexis. If you'd taken care of Veerka for me, I wouldn't have had to create this war."

My jaw remains slack as thousands of thoughts race through my mind. Veerka? How could she be a player in all of this? If this evil son of a bitch wanted her dead, it means there truly is goodness in her. It means she was someone standing in his way of taking over San Halos.

I'll figure out the Veerka situation after he spills the truth about his son and his implication with Rachel. And after I get out of here, I'll feed that rotten *warlock* kid to Rachel's iguana. Well, dragon.

With clenched teeth, I say, "So Zane is your son."

How can this be, anyway? How the hell did I not sense Jamieson's evil oozing off that kid? Any child of Jamieson must have been born from pure evil. But then, something else hits me—he's also the son of Devania, who stands against everything Jamieson believes in. What I'd like to know is if this kid obtained any of Devania's traits. While Jamieson might be a warlock, his mother is a Ukrisse demon, which means if Zane inherited her gifts, he can morph into anything or anyone, making it almost impossible to track him.

Jamieson leans back again, his chair squeaking. He grins, almost childlike, then snaps forward and plants his elbows on his knees. "It's brilliant, wouldn't you agree? My relationship with the vampires remains intact, and the person who will take the fall for this is my son's bitch of a mother, Devania."

I feel like an absolute moron. How did I not foresee any of this? And what's Zane doing with Rachel? Has he harmed her? Is he planning on hurting her? I need to find her.

"Your little witch is the one person capable of breaking our blood spell, and, well, that problem's already being taken care of."

This time, I lunge so hard that both of my forearms' radius bones snap upward, tearing through the skin of my arm. Refusing to show any sign of pain, I bite my tongue and hold my breath.

Jamieson winces and lets out a high-pitched whistle. "That must've hurt."

The pain doesn't bother me—I'm used to it. Besides, my arms will heal in a matter of seconds. What hurts me the most is knowing that Rachel is in danger and that I don't know how to help her.

Drax takes a step forward, likely on instinct, and Jamieson raises a stiff finger. "Unless you want to become a pile of hot guts, I suggest you remain where you are, boy."

He hesitates, and I can see the pain in his eyes. It reminds me of the first time I met Drax, and how terrified he was of me when I came to his defense. Three vampires were bullying him in his hometown, throwing him against moss-covered cobblestones and swinging their fists at his face.

Although the feebles couldn't see him—I could.

That wide-eyed look he gave me told me he'd grown up thinking he was nothing more than a waste of skin. Reptilian Humanoids aren't often known for having low self-esteem. While they may not possess magic, they are incredibly strong and some even morph into dragon-like beasts.

Drax, however, flinched the moment I stepped toward him. He scurried behind a pile of garbage and hid his face from the light of nearby sconces, his pointed horns poking out between the cracks of his fingers. It was like he was ashamed for not having been able to stand up for himself.

And as he stares at me now, it's obvious that all he wants to do is save me the way I saved him all those years ago.

"Well, isn't that interesting," Jamieson says with his fingers curled around his chin. His gaze lingers on my arms, which have already healed. "What are you, anyway? Krin? A Zykrr demon?" Then, his eyes widen slightly. "Or could you possibly be an Immortalus demon?"

I fight the urge to scoff. If there's anything as ridiculous as the name Immortalus, it's the demon itself. It's more of a myth than anything since no one has ever come forward to share an encounter. Some people believe that if an Immortalus grants you the power of immortality—that's the only power it has, which I assume it exchanges for money—a contract is created stating that neither their identity, nor their gift, can ever be spoken of again. To what extent this is reinforced, no one knows, but there have been cases of certain feebles who never grow old, and one day, out of nowhere, they die without any known cause—maybe after having spoken of their exchange. Who knows?

Holding my breath, I glower at Jamieson. The thing about Immortalus demons is that not many people know about them. And those who do are either super old or proficient in demonology. So the question is, how much does this Jamieson know? How dangerous is he, really?

Although I want nothing more than to slit his

throat and spoon-feed him his blood, I have to play this carefully. Slowly, I straighten my posture, bow my head, and offer the most seductive smile I can conjure.

"Oh, Jamieson," I say, projecting my Lure onto him.

But before I can get another word in, he whips his hand sideways, causing an electric-like ball to fizzle in the air. Then, he shakes his head at me like a disappointed teacher. "Nice try, Alexis. And I should have known, with that beauty of yours. I suppose I never imagined succubus demons to be so, well, forceful. I always envisioned a feminine beauty."

What the fuck is that supposed to mean?

Calm down, Alexis. There are matters way more important than Jamieson's perspective of you. Besides, gender doesn't matter to you. If he thinks you're a masculine beauty, hell—beauty's beauty. Maybe that's how he rolls.

I'm stunned by my self-reflection. How am I so clear-minded right now? Ace is dead and Rachel's on her way to the same place. But in the back of my mind, all I can think about is the conversation I had with Ace.

Alexis, daughter of Eros and granddaughter of Ares and Aphrodite. I never understood the whole incest thing. Some historical documentation even suggests that Zeus was both the father and grandfather of Eros.

It sounds ridiculous, but there's a part of me that does believe I'm a demigod, and if I am the daughter of Eros, that would make me Cupid's daughter (depending on which historical timeframe you're researching), which is mind-blowing. It would explain a lot of unusual things that have happened in my past, and it would explain how I survived all the close encounters I've had with death. It's as if someone has been protecting me. Whether this person is Alice, my doll, Ace, or powerful beings overhead, I can't say for sure. But as I think of Eros, I feel whole and calm.

"Why is Zane with Rachel?" I ask.

Jamieson leans back into his chair and twiddles his thumbs. "Do you expect me to explain everything to you step by step?"

"Well, you probably should," I say. "Because I don't understand how a moron like you could pull any of this off, so I'm starting to think you're lying to me about everything."

He knits his brows.

If there's one way to light a fire under Jamieson's ass, it's by attacking his ego. Now, I have him right where I want him.

"You know nothing," he hisses. "You fae. You're a disgrace to the magical world."

I fight the urge to correct him by saying, *Technically, we're all shadow dwellers, which makes us one big family.* But it wouldn't change anything. He's a warlock, and most warlocks think that witches are weak and fae have no business being part of the Council of Elders.

"You allow a group of old witches and fae to make all the decisions for you. Councils debate too much. Decisions are rarely made."

I'm not sure why he's using the word *you*. It's not like I'm the one who makes any big decisions. And what's he going on about? From where I'm sitting, it sounds like he thinks a dictatorship would be more beneficial to the entire world of shadow dwellers. Let me guess: Jamieson would be the perfect candidate.

"And then, of course, I heard about the book. Well done, by the way. I should be thanking you for extracting it from its hiding place."

My throat swells as I'm reminded that Rachel being in danger is all my fault. Had I not stolen the *Book of Origin*, this would have never happened in the first place.

"Beatrix," he says plainly, as if this is supposed to mean something.

When I don't react, he rubs his chin. "So you don't know who she is."

"Am I supposed to?" I ask.

"No, I suppose not," he says. "Most people don't know anything about Zerachu's sister. Not even the vampires, which isn't all that surprising. They're a lot of brainless shells with sharp little teeth if you ask me."

I'm about to make some smart-ass remark like,

Let me guess, she's the evil twin sister, but I know better than to interrupt Jamieson when he's monologing. Besides, that could be exactly who she is. Isn't that how it always works? The big reveal ends up being someone's evil twin sibling… The one who got the least attention out of the two growing up.

So cliché.

Shaking his head, he smiles to himself. "She said it was the easiest thing she's ever done. You know, fooling Rachel into believing she was Zerachu. What was it she said? *Like taking candy from a baby.*

"So what does Veerka have to do with all of this?" I ask.

He uncrosses his legs and leans against his armrest. "I thought you were brighter than that, Alexis."

"Funny," I say. "I thought the same thing about you. Can't understand why Lucius's girlfriend is such a threat to you."

He squeezes the leather of his armrest so hard that it tears. "She's a block," he hisses, strands of his hair falling again as he shakes his head rigorously. "You see, love has a way of blinding those entranced by it, and Lucius, well, he's gotten weak. Veerka has made him weak."

All right, so now I have all the information that I need.

Jamieson orchestrated this whole thing with the help of his son, Zane, and Zerachu's sister,

Beatrix. Pretty simple. I'm tempted to ask him where the evil witch is, but I know Jamieson, and he won't waste his breath on any details that don't make him look like a genius. Telling me where Beatrix is hiding doesn't serve him, and the longer I sit here, the more at risk Rachel becomes. Besides, I have it all figured out. All I have to do is get Rachel back, along with Zerachu. With a blood spell, Zerachu can bring us to Beatrix to take back the *Book of Origin* and that talisman.

"Well, thanks for the chat," I say. "It's been nice."

He looks bemused, and with good reason. I'm talking like I'm about to make some grand escape, and although I have no idea if my plan is going to work, I have to try. If Eros was able to grant Ace the gift of teleportation, it means that somewhere deep inside of me, I have the potential to harness that same power.

Although this might be the dumbest time to test out my hypothesis, I have to give it all I have.

Closing my eyes, I inhale a deep breath and focus all of my energy on freeing myself from my cuffs, grabbing Drax, and returning to the Lucky Cheetah Motel. I might be going into this blind, but if I've learned anything about magic from being around Rachel, it's that concentration is key.

I imagine Drax's face and the texture of his scaly skin against my palms as I grab him; the motel's lingering stench of cigarette smoke; our room's missing roof and the overcast sky; Mr. Mushroom greeting me with wet kisses and a wagging stub for a tail; and Rachel's new pet iguana scurrying underneath the bed. For a moment, my mind shifts over to Ace, and a sharp pain radiates down my throat and into my chest.

Focus, Alexis.

"What the hell are you doing, Alexis?"

I ignore Jamieson's voice, along with the sound of a blade coming out of its sheath.

"It's unfortunate that it's come to this," he says. "I've heard the only way to kill a succubus is to cut off its head."

I seal my eyes even tighter as a burst of energy fills through me.

"Alexis, what are you doing?" Drax snaps.

I'm almost there—I can feel it.

"Don't worry," Jamieson says, his voice aimed at Drax. "You'll get your turn."

The sound of clothes chaffing fills the space in front of me, and although I refuse to open my eyes, I envision Jamieson standing in front of me with a sword over his head and a menacing scowl on his face.

You've got this, Alexis.

"Alexis!" Drax shouts, and then suddenly, a growl fills the room.

I snap my eyes open to find Drax lunging straight for Jamieson. His mouth, a huge gaping hole, reveals over a hundred razor-sharp teeth spinning in circles inside his mouth.

What the fuck?

Although his movements are fast, everything feels like it's going in slow motion. Jamieson turns toward his attacker, his sword held up in the air, and as Drax jumps, six-inch claws come tearing out of his fingertips and porcupine-like quills appear all over his body.

Now, all I see is a monster, with Drax nowhere to be found.

How did I not know about this? And why the fuck did he wait so long to morph? With twirling teeth, he reaches for Jamieson midair. But rather than slicing his sword at the lunging beast, Jamieson points his finger and shouts something.

In a flash, Drax disappears as if having never existed, and I blink over and over again in an attempt to convince my brain that he isn't gone. He can't be. Drax's my best friend, my brother. How did this happen? How the fuck did I allow this to happen?

I jerk from side to side. If I can't break free of the cuffs, I sure as hell can snap this chair into a thousand pieces. Screaming at the top of my lungs, I throw my arms upward, snapping the chair's armrests right off.

Instinctively, Jamieson takes a step back, no doubt sensing that he's about to die.

With my claws extracted, I lunge for his face. I've never wanted to kill anyone so badly before, but with this rage inside of me, I don't merely want to kill Jamieson; I want to obliterate him from the universe entirely.

Right as my claws are about to penetrate his throat, he shouts something incomprehensible, and everything around me disappears.

Chapter 4

"Alexis, wake up."

I recognize that voice. Am I dreaming? Or, am I hallucinating? The voice can't be real. It isn't possible.

"Alexis, get your ass up."

Okay, it's definitely real.

My eyes pop open to find Drax's scaly green face hovering inches away from mine. He smiles, revealing his reptilian teeth—nothing monstrous like what I just witnessed. Did I imagine it? Oh, shit. Am I dead? Did Jamieson cut off my head and send me into the afterlife?

I sit upright, feeling like the room is spinning around me.

"Drax?" I say.

He grins from ear to ear. What the hell does he have to be so happy about? What's going on?

I blink, rub my eyes, and look around.

Above me is the partial roof of our motel room, and beside me, Mr. Mushroom lies cuddled up on Riskus's lap. Riskus stares at me, his little goblin hands petting my dog's head.

I'm glad to see they're getting along.

And then it hits me. "Holy shit, I did it."

Drax's hairless brows meet above the bridge of his nose. "Did what?"

"Got us out of there!" I say like it's obvious. "I mean, the result was a little delayed, but... I fucking did it."

Drax gives me the *look*. With an arched brow, a crinkled nose, and his upper lip pulled over two of his sharp teeth, it's a look that tells me I'm saying something stupid, or I'm not understanding the reality of whatever is happening.

He doesn't do it often because I'm usually the one who's right, but when he does, I know something's up.

"What?" I say, twirling in circles. "What am I missing?"

Without a word, he waggles both eyebrows and points a finger at my shoulder.

Tucking my chin, I glance down at my right shoulder to find a small black cricket with two long antennas. It stares at me with its beady little eyes and I squeal, prepared to smack it off me.

"Don't hurt him!" Drax says.

The cricket chirps and I pull my face even farther away from it, adding several chins to my face. From this angle, it looks like a little alien. Ugh, bugs freak me out. You'd think after a thousand years, a girl would get used to having them around.

Nope—not me.

"What's going on?" I say.

The air from my mouth wiggles the cricket's antennas.

"Oh, I don't know," Drax says. "Maybe thank him?"

The room goes silent.

"Ace?" I say.

He doesn't respond, but it looks like he's trying to.

"He's the one who brought you here," Drax says. "He brought me, then went back for you."

"I was about to kill Jamieson!" I growl, causing Ace's antennas to fall flat on his head.

I stop bitching at once when I realize I'm yelling at a cricket. So instead, I stick my index finger on my shoulder and Ace climbs on. But as I pull away, he slips off my finger and falls toward the floor. I catch him right in time, holding him in the palm of my hand.

"What's wrong with him?" I ask.

Drax shrugs. "He's probably drained. Doesn't it take energy for him to teleport or something? And imagine at that size. In all honesty, I don't know how he did it."

"You're alive," I breathe, an unfamiliar sense of relief washing over me. "How—"

"He must have teleported right before Jamieson's foot crushed him. But he won't be alive for long if we don't do something," Drax says.

My eyes shoot up at him. "Like what, genius? I'm not having sex with a fucking cricket."

There's the look again.

"That wasn't even on my mind," he says. "Wow, Alexis. Just... wow."

I make my eyelids go flat. He can be condescending all he wants, but the truth of the matter is that Ace is an incubus, and although healing comes naturally to us demons, it's impossible if we're depleted of energy. And the sole way for us to get that energy is by feeding off sexual energy.

My eyes dart toward Riskus. "Can you do anything?" I ask.

He slants his brows and shakes his head. "I–I'm sorry. I only know some magic," he says, his high-pitched voice making Ace go crazy in my hand. "I do not know how to transform someone."

"Fuck," I mutter. "We need Rachel." At once, everything Jamieson said comes back to me. "And she needs us."

In a panic, I storm through our motel room. "Gotta be something," I mutter.

I can sense everyone's eyes on me, but I don't care. I force my way through the broken wall and search Ace's room, throwing blankets into the air and pulling out drawers with one hand.

When at last I reach the last oak drawer of his room's dresser, I find something I can use.

I reach for the small rectangular box and open

it. Inside are some hair clips and a necklace. "This should work," I say to myself, emptying the box of its contents.

On top of the dresser is a dusty box of Kleenex. I pluck one out, lay inside the box, and drop Ace overtop of it. He flops on his back, his little legs barely moving, and my throat swells. "Don't worry, I have a plan. Hang in there a little longer, okay?"

He doesn't respond—not like he can.

"It's going to be dark, and maybe bumpy, but it's temporary."

And with that, I close the box, lock the latch, and rush back into the other room, careful not to shake the box too much.

"Riskus," I exclaim, and he flinches. "You carry some kind of magical powder on you, right?"

He nods, but the way his oversized nose wrinkles tells me he's afraid of what I'm about to ask.

"You know Rachel better than anyone," I say, "which means you must have learned a thing or two from her."

One of his eyes goes bigger than the other.

"I need you to create a portal that leads me right to her."

His jaw loosens, revealing small incisor teeth.

"Are you insane?" Drax says. "He isn't a witch."

"No," I say, "but he knows magic. He has that ability. We don't."

"That doesn't mean he can create a portal!"

Drax scoffs.

"What other option do we have?" I say. "Rachel's in danger, and without her, Ace is as good as dead. If we don't do anything, we lose them both."

"Rachel is in danger?" Riskus squeals, and I feel Ace bounce around inside the box.

I nod.

Drax bites his lower lip. A few months ago, neither one of us would have considered going through with this. We've always been selfish, living with the ideology that people, for the most part, are inherently bad and don't deserve the time of day.

But Rachel's grown on us, and so has Ace. In a sense, they've become part of our fucked-up little family.

"Well?" I say.

Drax sighs. "All right, it's worth a shot."

Grinning, I turn to Riskus. "Can you do this, or what?"

He looks terrified with his upside-down smile and fidgety hands, but for Rachel, he'll give it his best shot.

Chapter 5

The portal looks nothing like the ones Rachel usually creates. It's yellow, zaps every few seconds, and even spits out what appear to be particles of dust. Inside the hole, it looks like a giant vortex that's going to swallow me up, shred me to pieces, and send me off into space.

Okay, I'm freaked out.

"What's the worst that could happen?" I say, more so to myself than anyone else.

Emotionless, Riskus says, "Well, there are several things that could happen. You could disintegrate, or even—"

"It was rhetorical, Riskus," I say, not wanting to hear any more of these *possibilities*. "I'm sure you did your very best."

He tightens his lips and doesn't make a peep.

Drax clears his throat. "You can answer that one, Riskus. You did your best, right?"

He perks up. "For Rachel, yes."

I don't bother asking him if he would have put less effort into this if Rachel wasn't involved because it doesn't matter. The portal's created, and if all goes well, it'll take me straight to Rachel.

"If I don't come back," I say, turning to Drax.

"Don't waste your breath on some speech," he cuts me off. "I'm going with you."

I raise a palm. "No, you need to stay here in case—"

"In case what, Alexis? Riskus is watching Mr. Mushroom and they're safe. I may not have been much use to you back there, but that was the second time in my life I morphed, and the first time wasn't pretty."

"What are you saying?" I ask.

Pinching his wide, flat nose, he says, "I was raised to believe that I was nothing more than a killing machine. My parents pushed and pushed until one day, I snapped and shifted, just like they wanted me to. Kept saying it was part of our bloodline. That eating people was how we survived. I guess my anger got the best of me, and I went after anyone I could see." He averts his gaze, no doubt replaying that horrific day in his mind. "But I'm not angry anymore. And I didn't realize it until what happened back there with Jamieson. I can control it, Alexis. I didn't think I could, but the moment Ace brought me back to the motel and I saw Riskus and Mr. Mushroom, I shifted back." He places his hands on his hips like Superman. "Let me come with you. I can help."

Drax isn't wrong. What he turned into—

whatever that was—was a killing machine. I wish I'd known about it sooner, but I understand why Drax kept it a secret for so long. In his mind, that creature inside of him was nothing more than a soulless killing machine. The real monster was his family.

"All right," I say, breaking the silence. "You can come with, but if you get hurt, I'll kill you myself."

He rolls his eyes.

Slowly, I turn toward the spinning portal, and for a moment, I consider changing my mind. Am I being an idiot? Riskus is no witch. There's a possibility that I might end up somewhere really messed up, or nowhere at all.

My biggest worry, aside from disappearing into oblivion, is moving into another dimension. It looks cool in movies and TV shows, but it hurts like hell and messes with your body big-time. Scientifically speaking, all of your cells have to change the pattern and speed of their vibration to match those of the new dimension.

It isn't pretty, that's for sure.

I've done it a handful of times and each time, I lie on the ground, unable to move for at least a week. On the bright side, there was a time when a mesmerizing hybrid being with long red hair, piercing yellow eyes, and tribal tattoos all over her body found me. She dragged me through the mud without any difficulty at all. It was in the middle of a blue leaf forest, and as I slid through the mud, colorful flowers reached for me, either wanting to help me or to grab me for themselves.

The creature brought me inside her home and placed me on her small, wooden bed. Crouching, she examined me by pulling and prodding at my hair, my face, and my clothes until finally, she decided to strip me down to examine every inch of me.

It was kind of hot.

Especially when she discovered that I had an entry point that wasn't my mouth.

Drax clears his throat and I snap out of it. He gives me a stern look and jerks his head toward the portal.

Great. Now I'm hungry. Let's hope wherever I'm going, I can find someone to feed off of.

"Are we doing this, or what?" he says.

I glance back at Mr. Mushroom, who's standing on all fours on the bed with a wagging butt and perked ears. He barks, drops his front legs, and barks again.

Is he trying to warn me against going?

I shake the thought. How would he know where I'm going, or what's going to happen? He's probably worried.

I blow him a kiss and this seems to calm him. "I'll be back, little man. You sit tight."

And with that, I close my eyes, clench my teeth, and throw myself into the portal.

Chapter 6

The smell of rot and feces fills my nose before my ears catch the sound.

At first, it's faint, but the oinking evolves into what sounds like an orchestra of pigs. Some are high-pitched, others deeper and bubbly sounding. But it doesn't take a genius to know I've landed right in the middle of a pigpen.

Damn it, Riskus.

"Drax?" I whisper.

He doesn't respond. Even if he did, it would be impossible to hear him over the sound of all these pigs.

I'm about to stand up when an icy hand grabs me by the wrist and pulls me flat on my back.

"What the f—" I start, but I'm too taken aback by the sight next to me to give anyone lip.

Dirt covers the man, or woman, from head to toe, the whites of their big brown eyes creating a contrast between every blink. I part my lips again, but the mud-man, or mud-woman, raises a finger over what I assume are their lips.

That's when the trembling starts.

It feels like an earthquake, only far too consistent to be caused by Gaia.

Every few seconds, the ground shakes and the pigs squeal in response. I'd be lying if I said I wasn't anxious. It feels like something big is walking toward us.

And when I say big, I mean *really* big.

Above us is a red sky that looks like someone painted it in blood. There's no solid roof or ceiling to protect us from whatever the hell is coming. All that's protecting us is a wooden fence constructed of sanded logs, and a roofless enclosure full of hay bales.

Really, Riskus? Where the fuck did you send me?

The trembling in the earth gets so intense that pigs start running all over the place. One manages to land on my rib, cracking it instantly. I wince, but I don't move. If this mud-person is trying to keep me safe, it means they've been here a while. And if that's the case, how injured are they? How does anyone survive lying underneath a horde of pigs?

Another snap.

This time, it's my ankle.

As they run around and over me, creating a blur of pinks and browns, a small opening appears every few seconds. Through it, I glimpse the monster moving toward us.

"You have got to be kidding me," I say.

Several *shhh*'s echo around me.

How many people are hiding in here? It doesn't matter. Right now, all that matters is that giant cyclops marching toward us. It looks the same as your stereotypical cyclopes portrayed in video games or movies. Its skin, a grayish beige, seems to be centuries old and wraps around its giant muscles and overhanging belly. It's one eyeball, about the size of a huge tractor wheel, rolls in every direction as if trying to determine what it wants to eat today. Although I can't measure the thing from here, I'd describe it as being three times the size of a Tyrannosaurus rex. In its right hand is a spiked club that it drags by its side, breaking boulders and trees in its path.

Given that it doesn't have massive, sagging breasts, I can tell it's male.

Why am I just lying here? The smart thing to do would be to get up and fly. And if I wanted to be badass, I'd fly over his head, drop down and shoot the fucker in the eye with my Glocks. Cyclopes are pretty useless without their eye. But I can't move, and I don't know what I'm dealing with yet, and if I propel myself into the air, other creatures could target me.

Let's see how this plays out.

As the cyclops moves closer, its eye gets bigger and bigger. He stares at the panicking pigs, bends forward, and reaches a slow-moving hand toward the animals. Shrieks and squeals fill the red sky as the cyclops's massive fingers draw nearer. He's about to scoop up a gray-spotted pig when his giant eyeball focuses on something else—someone else.

A rotten smile splits his ugly face in half as he reaches for his new target. Although I can't see what the cyclops is going for, I'm guessing he spotted a person's face.

Then, the screaming explodes all around us, and out from the pigpen comes a short, petite-looking woman with legs kicking and mouth wide open. The cyclops is indifferent to her suffering, and to shut her up, squeezes his giant fingers around her torso. Cracking and snapping fills the air as the cyclops pulls back, and the woman's legs hang limp outside of his fist.

A young man next to me shifts violently like he's preparing to attack the cyclops, but several muddy hands grab him around the face, neck, and torso. He's about to scream, but another hand covers his mouth, allowing only moans to escape.

But the cyclops doesn't seem to care. He's too preoccupied with his new toy to care about the pen. Proud of his catch of the day, he turns around and stomps back toward the castle with the crushed body in his right hand.

"There's nothing you can do," someone hisses.

"You'll get yourself killed."

"Patricia," the man cries. "How did this happen? She... she was..." He drops his face into the mud, sobbing uncontrollably.

"What the fuck is going on here?" I interrupt. Given what happened moments ago, I might sound callous, but I need answers and I need them now.

The woman lying closest to the sobbing man—an Asian woman with long black hair, filthy skin, and cracked pale lips—spits mud from her mouth. "We call this place the Kingdom of Shadows," she says solemnly. "No one knows where it is. It seems to be made of magic."

"What's the point of it?" I ask.

An older gentleman speaks up. His face is so muddy I can't make out a single feature. "We ain't certain. The four of us have been here for, well, can't even say. We seen many people come and go. And when I say go, I mean get grabbed by that thing you saw. It don't always kill people, either. It sniffs them before deciding whether or not to crush 'em. A few are kept alive and taken to the castle. If it don't find anyone, he takes a pig. And there are always plenty o' pigs to take. It's like they keep appearin' to give us the illusion of safety."

This makes little sense. What kind of sick game is this? If the portal worked, and if Zerachu and Rachel are here, then I assume this place is for housing prisoners. But why kill some people, and not others? And what's with the pigs? Something fucked up is going on.

"Are you all fae?" I ask.

The group nods.

"Drax?" I call out. "Have any of you seen a green

man?"

This must sound crazy, but I'm not sure how else to describe him.

"Drax?" I try again, panic in my voice.

I'm about to get up when the older gentleman says, "Ain't no use tryin' to go lookin' for him, ma'am. We didn't see anyone else appear but you. And if you try to get out of the pen, well, you won't be able to. It's magic or somethin' surroundin' us. You'll light up in flames the second you try to cross the fence. Only way anyone gets outta here is dead or in that cyclops's hand, and even then, that's a gamble."

How is that possible? How did I end up here without Drax? We entered the same portal.

"Did any of you see a young girl?" I ask.

The older gentleman locks eyes with the Asian woman next to him and he nods. "As a matter o' fact, we did. But she done something we've never seen before."

"What do you mean?" I ask.

"She came with a boy about the same age," he says. "And then that boy took her by the hand and walked on out o' here and straight for the castle. Wasn't hurt by the magic or nothin'."

I clench my teeth.

Zane.

If Zane has free rein in this sick, fucked-up little kingdom, then he or his father created it. What I'd like to know, though, is the location of this kingdom. We can't be in another dimension—I'd have felt that. The cool, crisp air around us reminds me of the Dark Hall. Wherever we are, it was created by magic, and if Jamieson is the one who created this place, there's no telling how much more fucked up things are about to get.

"So the girl's in the castle?" I ask, matter-of-factly.

The group nods again, and the gentleman says, "Is she a friend of yours?"

"Yeah," I say. "So I need to get inside that castle."

The gentleman's eyes soften, reminding me of a sweet grandfather. "I'm sorry, ma'am, but we can't help ya. What you're asking is impossible."

The others seem to agree. The sobbing man looks up at me from behind red, bloodshot eyes and inches away. It's like he thinks I'm going to get the rest of them killed.

"How often does this cyclops come?" I ask.

"Every sunset," says the Asian woman.

As she says that, the red overcast sky darkens to a bloody crimson and the pigs grow quieter.

"In the morning, the pig keepers will come," she continues. "They'll throw food inside the pen, but don't go for it. While they're not allowed to kill you, they'll do everything in their power to help the cyclops see you. It's better if they don't know we're here." She pauses and averts her gaze. "If there's anything left after the pigs have eaten, we can share it."

I have no intention of eating disgusting leftovers tossed into a pigpen.

The only thing I give a shit about is getting inside that castle, and that's what I'm going to do.

Chapter 7

The sunrise reminds me of a highly edited image of Mars.

The entire pen fills up with a bright, blinding red as the oversized sun penetrates the sky. The sun itself is a candy apple red, making me want to stack on three pairs of sunglasses.

A soft wind slips through the log fence, whistling as it sweeps through all the pigs. I wait to hear roosters crowing or hens ceremoniously crying out after laying their eggs, but aside from the pigs' footsteps around my head, I don't hear a thing.

I'm not on some farmland where chickens flap their wings and cows frolic in the fields. Some sadistic prick designed this place intentionally. Beyond the pen, I can't see much. Every time I try to observe my surroundings, the sun's hot rays make my eyes water. You'd think it was created this way to prevent prisoners from even considering escape.

Not that we could, anyways—according to my

fellow prisoners, a magic barrier has us all trapped inside this dump. Squinting, I gaze toward the north, where the castle sits without flaw. Luscious green grass surrounds its perimeter, unlike here, where everything around us looks like either dirt or blood.

Sighing, I inhale the stench of pig shit and close my eyes.

The cyclops comes every evening, which means this is going to be a long day.

I pass the time by counting curly tails around me, and occasionally opening Ace's wooden box to check on him. He's still alive, but he looks rough.

Shit. Ace.

I have two options: I can either hide him in the pen, or I can take him inside with me. The problem with taking him inside is that I risk his box getting crushed if the cyclops decides to turn my insides to a pulp. But if I leave him here, there's no telling how long it'll take me to get back, *if* I can even get back.

I play numerous scenarios over in my mind as the sun rises higher and higher until finally, the sound of footsteps approaches. It's accompanied by the sound of metal clanging—assumedly swords and shields.

It must be the guards.

As instructed, I add more mud to my face and don't move when they make their way over to the pen. Thankfully, my fellow prisoners showed me a few good hiding spots where the pigs don't tend to go.

"Ya think any of 'em are hidin' in there?" says one of the guards.

His voice is nasal, so much so that I imagine him being five feet tall and skinnier than me—the kind of guy TV producers like to cast as IT department employees.

The other guard scoffs. "Who cares? Krusher'll get 'em if they are. Ain't that right? Ya good for nothin' roaches! I hope Krusher tears ya to shreds, ya hear me?"

His voice is a bit deeper—not by much, but enough for me to create an imaginary version of him in my mind: he's my height, toned but not muscular, and has a goatee. Why? Because it gives him a false sense of manliness, as if growing a patch of hair on his face also causes an abundance of testosterone to flow from his marble-sized balls.

Fucking useless prick.

And why is he trying to provoke us? Don't they have better things to do than to taunt helpless prisoners who are hiding in pig shit?

It takes everything in me not to open my eyes and tell them to go fuck themselves. I'm not the type to keep quiet, especially where bullying is concerned, but I remind myself that keeping my mouth shut is what I need to do to find Rachel, save Ace, and figure out where Drax disappeared to.

I hope to the gods he didn't end up in the castle. It's doubtful, though. Whatever this place is, I'm sure it's designed to ensure that any new guests end up in the pen first.

Suddenly, the pigs squeal and oink, rushing to one spot. The weight of their steps shakes the ground under me, causing bits of dirt and shit to roll down my face and tickle my nose.

"Heeeeere, piggy piggy," says Goatee.

Then, something loud snaps, and a pig squeals out in pain.

Goatee laughs hysterically as the pigs run around in a panic. I clench my teeth, reminding myself to stay out of it. Even if I do get up and go after them, I'll never reach them. Not with that barrier in the way. I assume they can pass through it as they wish, while we, mere guests in this realm, have no power whatsoever.

I could try to Lure them—I'd love nothing more—but it's a risk.

For once, I'll do what I'm told and sit tight.

They leave at last, and the moment they're gone, I burst out of my hiding spot and rush over to where the food is. Behind me, a few voices hiss at me, telling me to stop.

I wasn't born yesterday—they want the food for themselves. I'm an added mouth to feed, and I'm also the newbie, which means I should be the one who eats last, if at all. But I'm not rushing over to the food for me. That's not what I'm hungry for, anyways.

"What are you doing?" says the sobbing man

from yesterday. "You have no right!" He no longer sounds sad. The hostility in his voice makes it sound like he's prepared to attack me if it means getting a bite to eat.

While these people may have protected me from the cyclops last night, people are still people, and when it comes to survival, beings are designed to survive at all costs.

As I crawl through the mud, I come across two moldy, half-eaten loaves of bread, slimy blueberries, soggy lettuce, and other mush that I can't make out. I grab the bread and throw it back to my fellow prisoners, who instantly stop bickering about me.

Instead, I reach for a few blueberries and pinch some of the colorful mush. Like a soldier in the trenches, I crawl back to the gang, roll over on my back, and pull Ace's wooden box out from my belt.

"What is that?" asks the guy who was yelling at me moments ago.

"A friend," I say plainly. I crack open the box, smile down at Ace, and place the blue slime inside.

The three of them exchange confused glances, and rightfully so. I'm caring for a cricket. Who in their right mind does that? Then again, I shouldn't be judging. As much as bugs gross the shit out of me, life is life, no matter the size.

"It's a long story," I say. "He's not actually a cricket."

When I feel something sharp rub against the

back of my head, I reach for it. Out from my muddy, chaotic hair comes a large, salted pretzel. The gang stares at me with large, desperate eyes.

"Here," I say, handing it to the Asian woman.

She snatches it as if her life depends on it, but then hesitates, splits it into four, and gives everyone a piece. I tell her I'm okay, and she eats my piece. I feel awful for these people. How long have they been here? Will they even survive?

Probably not.

I lean against a small bale of hay and watch the shadows rotate around a wooden post as the sun starts its slow descent.

"You guys seem like decent people," I say, "so I'm going to tell you my plan so you don't freak out and think I'm dead."

They're confused. They barely know me, and I'm talking to them like we're friends. Although we haven't known each other long, I feel as though we have, which I'm certain has something to do with us surviving this shithole together.

"I'm a succubus," I say.

No one seems bothered by my comment, so I add, "That means I'm immortal. Well, for the most part."

This seems to capture their attention. Many people have a misconception about fae and immortality. They think because most fae don't age, they can't die, which couldn't be farther from the truth. I know many fae who lived to be over a hundred years old, only to one day get run over by a horse carriage or die in a tragic war.

The older gentleman rubs his dirty chin and scratches at his gray hair. "You ain't gonna try to sneak into my sleep, are ya? My old ticker ain't what it used to be."

"What? No. I'm not going after any of you," I cut him off. "Besides, I never mastered the whole attacking people in their sleep thing."

He looks disappointed.

I roll my eyes. "I'm gonna let the cyclops catch me."

All three of them gasp, sounding like a giant suction cup.

"Are you insane?" says the younger man. "There's a reason that monster's name is *Krusher*. You understand that, right?"

"I never said it wouldn't be painful," I say.

The Asian woman's eyes narrow on me curiously. "My gods. Why would you do such a thing?"

For Rachel, that's why.

"Don't worry about me," I say. "I'm letting you know so you don't get upset when it happens."

"But why—" the woman tries.

"Listen, I told you my plan to ease any guilt you might feel when it happens, but I won't explain everything to you. If I can find a way to get you guys out of here once I've done what I came here to do, I will."

I feel stupid as the words come out of my mouth, like I'm trying to be some heroic big shot. That's not what I'm trying to do. Honestly, these people aren't my problem, but I'm already going into the castle on a rescue mission, so if getting them out after that isn't much more work, why wouldn't I do it? I'd be a pretty shitty person not to.

Everyone goes quiet for what feels like hours as the sun lowers and a breeze sweeps through the pen. Any minute now, that ugly creature is going to come crawling out from behind the castle and start stomping across the field to fetch a new prize.

I wish he'd hurry up already.

I smirk, realizing how insane I might sound if I were ever to vocalize these thoughts to anyone. Who wants to get crushed by some giant? Will it hurt? Of course it will. It'll be excruciating—so much so, that part of me thinks I'm being an idiot for even considering this.

But what choice do I have? The world needs Zerachu, I need to save Rachel, Ace needs either one of those two to change back, and I need Ace to find Drax.

There isn't much of a choice here.

Everyone I care about is relying on me to save them somehow, some way.

Oh, man. I *am* being heroic. How nauseating.

As the sun disappears halfway behind the horizon, the ground beneath us trembles. Eyes pop out from behind a bale of hay. It's as if they're experiencing this for the first time. I suppose it's a normal reaction. How could anyone become desensitized to a giant cyclops reaching inside a pigpen to grab a fae? If I weren't immortal, I'd be shitting myself.

Though I'd never admit this aloud, I'm scared.

I've broken many bones in my life—often many at once—but I've never been crushed before. How long will it take to recover?

The trembling gets louder and stronger, and my heartbeat quickens.

You're fucking crazy, Alexis.

I swallow, my throat sticking to itself as the monster gets closer and closer. He takes one slow step at a time, his sandaled feet making me even more nauseous. His big toenails, two gray and yellow slabs of rot, look about the size of freaking surfboards.

For Rachel.

I breathe out hard, as if this will somehow boost my confidence, and stand up.

It's only pain. You'll be fine.

I've never been much afraid of pain, but this is some next-level shit. This monster, should he decide to crush me, will turn my insides to soup and snap every bone in my body.

I may not be completely right in the head, but if the idea of getting pancaked didn't scare me in the slightest, it would be safe to say that I have severe psychological problems.

The creature's fat belly jiggles as he stomps his way over, dragging a spiked club beside him as he did the night prior.

"Well, wish me luck," I say.

No one wishes me luck. Everyone closes their eyes, the mud over their lids causing them to blend effortlessly with their surroundings. I, on the other hand, stand up and walk right into the middle of the pen.

In an instant, the cyclops's eye goes bigger, if that's even possible, and his rotten mouth stretches into a creepy smile. He shouts something incomprehensible, slaps his chest, and lets out a roar so loud the hair on my head flows backward.

Fuck.

I can't tell if I've excited the thing or pissed him off.

Not that it matters. I don't have the time to figure out what this brainless beast is thinking. The stomping evolves to jogging, and the ground shakes so violently that I have to bend my knees to keep from falling.

"This is it," I say to myself.

But then, I remember something—Ace.

Without hesitating, I tear the box off my belt, open it up, and pluck him out. "You aren't going to like this any more than me," I say, talking to the cricket in my palm, "but it's the only way."

"Argooosa!" the cyclops shouts, whatever the fuck that means.

My legs wobble as he takes the last few strides toward the pen, and at the same time, I throw Ace into my mouth and onto my tongue. He sits in the middle without moving, and I gag as his little antennas tickle the roof of my mouth.

The cyclops' huge, mold-encrusted hand comes sweeping toward me and I clench my teeth around Ace, forming a protective barrier. No matter what happens, I can't unclench my jaw. Why? Because I'm about to be shaken around in all sorts of directions, which means he'll be bouncing around in my mouth. If I unclench, I may bite down again when my bones start snapping, and if he's at the wrong place at the wrong time... Well, you get the picture.

The moment the cyclops's fingers wrap around my body, my head bounces back violently—a movement so abrupt that something loud snaps, and a sharp pain radiates down my back.

Fucking asshole. He hasn't even done his sniffing inspection and he's already injuring his catch.

He raises me, wind whistling through the cracks of his fingers, and brings me closer to the sky. With his other hand, the monster grabs me by the right leg.

My shin breaks the moment he grabs it and a soft cry echoes in my mouth, but I don't unclench my teeth.

He dangles me upside down, brings me close to

his bulblike nose, and takes in a big whiff. My hair gets pulled toward him, as do I, but he holds onto my broken shin tight enough for me not to get sucked into his hairy nostrils.

"No mageesh," he grunts.

What the fuck is he talking about? Then, without warning, he tosses me into the air, and as I'm about to pull out my wings and say *fuck it* to this whole undercover mission, his left hand catches me, crushing me instantly.

CHAPTER 8

No words can describe what it feels like to have your entire body crushed as an immortal. For the first time in my life, I wish I were a feeble. The idea of dying would ease me more than knowing I'm going to survive this. Do I even want to survive? Right now, no; I want to die.

My head rolls back as I slip in and out of consciousness.

It's physical pain, Alexis. Nothing more. You will survive this. You always do.

Shut the fuck up, my inner thoughts snap back.

They say there's nothing wrong with talking to yourself so long as you don't respond, but whoever said that must have been one hell of a lonely person.

I wince as my broken ribs puncture my lung, but I refuse to unclench my jaw. Next, a kidney explodes, and then worst of all, my liver tears.

Liver. Alcohol. Fuck.

Angry Rachel.

Rachel.

You're doing this for Rachel.

My thoughts come together like the broken words of a caveman. I remind myself that this pain is temporary, and I *will* recover—I *will* finish what I came here to do.

Nearby, the sound of something heavy erupts over rambunctious voices. I'm too weak and dazed by pain to open my eyes, but if I were to guess, I'd assume that guards were opening a set of iron gates.

Where are we? The back of the castle? Where's this big bastard taking me, anyway? Suddenly, I notice that my plan has a flaw. What happens if he intends to eat me? The second he bites off my head, I'm done for.

Fuck.

Cyclopes are known for eating humans. Was I seriously too hell-bent on getting inside the castle to consider this outcome?

For the first time in as long as I can remember, I ask whatever powers there might be to spare me. Shouldn't my biological dad be protecting me or something?

What's left of my stomach sinks as the cyclops moves his clenched fist closer to the ground. With my head dangling at the edge of his thumb, I crack my eyes open. His face, fuzzy and barely visible, seems to get more and more blurry no matter how many times I blink.

What is he doing? Where is he taking me?

Not too far. The sound of sharp metal scraping leather—maybe swords being pulled from sheaths—and loud authoritative male voices carry through the air.

"Slowly, slowly—"

Krusher grumbles something incoherent as if he's displeased with the orders he's being given. And who can blame him? The monster could crush the entire castle if he wanted to. From his perspective, he's being bossed around by little humans with toothpicks for swords and bread-thin armor. Why doesn't he kill them all? Someone powerful must have control over him.

And anyone capable of controlling a cyclops of that size is someone you don't want to fuck with.

At once, he loosens his grip, and my squished organs move around inside my body. I inhale slowly—it's excruciating given the fact that I have one lung left. Right now, the most important thing for me to do is to pretend that I'm dead. Any second now, I could lose function of my one good lung, and although it may not kill me, my body will react and I'll give myself away.

Without warning, Krusher drops me and a soft oomph comes out of my one lung. Fortunately, the guards nearby were too busy scurrying toward me to hear anything. When they pick me up, it takes everything in me not to shout out in pain. My organs, now Jell-O, swish around inside my body along with fragments of bone and bits of torn muscles.

The ground beneath us trembles as the cyclops walks away and I'm left lying on the grass next to a few castle guards.

"Pile's getting a little big," one of them says. "We should have let Krusher take this one. He's getting irritable. We haven't let him keep one in weeks."

"You know the rules," comes a stern voice. "She wants all of them. Once she finds what she's looking for, Krusher can go back to eating as many prisoners as he wants."

She? Who's *she?* The big boss? I'd be lying if I said I wasn't intrigued. I have a thing for bad girls. They tend to like it rough in bed, which gives me one hell of a charge. But the thought of having my way with an evil bitch dissipates when I'm reminded of my mission.

This woman may be responsible for what's happening, and *that* is anything but hot.

They lift me into the air and place me on a wooden platform. Based on what I've seen in this kingdom, I assume it's something as simple as a wagon. There doesn't seem to be any electricity or technology around here.

Gently, I move my tongue to the side of my mouth and feel around for Ace to make sure I didn't accidentally swallow him. To my great relief, he's still there, though he feels rigid and isn't moving. I'm running out of time.

"Right there," says one of the guards.

I'm raised into the air like a bag of dirt and thrown on something both firm and squishy. My teeth squeak as I bite down harder, holding my breath to stop myself from crying out in pain.

The voices fade as the guards' heavy boots hit the floor until finally, I'm left in silence.

Ew. What is this place?

A putrid sweet and sour smell fills my nostrils, making me want to vomit out what's left of my stomach. I'd know that scent anywhere—I've smelled it hundreds of times.

Decay.

Where am I?

The room is cool and damp, likely made of cement. I don't have to open my eyes to know I'm lying atop a pile of dead bodies. Bones jab me in the back, but I'm too weak to move.

Even opening one eye feels like an Olympic endeavor.

But finally, my right one snaps open, and my blurry vision begins to regain focus. If there's one thing I want to focus my energy on, it's replenishing my eyesight. It's important I know where I am and what's going on if I plan on getting out of here.

As presumed, the room is constructed of cement—from the floor to the walls to the ceiling. A small rectangular window sits high up on the right wall, almost touching the ceiling. Over it are iron bars forming a cross, no doubt to prevent any idiot from trying to climb out, even though the hole is about the size of a small raccoon.

Through the window comes a dark red light, which tells me the sun is almost set. It blends with the countless bloodstains on the floor, making the space look like it was once used as a blood pool. At the front of the room is a door constructed of old wood and rusty metal. The latch looks broken, which tells me I'm not locked inside.

Why would I be? This room is being used to store dead bodies—not live ones.

As much as I want to stand up, crack the door open, and investigate further, I can't. It's as if my body's given up on me.

How long will my recovery take? Typically, a wound or a broken bone heals within seconds. If the injury is severe enough, it can take up to a few hours. But a full-body crush? This is new to me. Not only must my body repair broken bones, tendons, and cartilage—it has to regrow certain organs.

I'm screwed.

I pass the time falling in and out of consciousness as the red light shining through the window disappears entirely, before reemerging the following morning. In the distance, people lament, but the sound doesn't last long. When this happens, a guard typically shouts something, and the whining stops.

Prisoners? It must be. The room I'm lying in looks like it used to be an isolation unit. A sharp pain shoots through my chest and something pops.

Yay—my second lung is back.

The healing goes on for hours, days, I can't tell. Maybe it hasn't even been a day. I'm about to attempt to raise my head when a loud sound fills the room and the door blasts open. I shut my eyes.

"Another useless one," a guard says.

That voice.

Without warning, someone throws a heavy body right on top of me, and all the air I managed to accumulate inside my new lungs blasts out.

"She wants a girl," the same voice says.

Is that Goatee? The prick from earlier?

"So take her," comes a small, nasal voice.

I know that voice, too. It's the two guards from before—the two assholes who kept provoking the pigs.

"We can't take from the top, Lynell, you know that," barks Goatee.

Are they talking about me?

Goatee continues. "You gotta problem followin' instructions, don't ya? Ain't rocket science. No bodies older than five days in here. You wanna be the one to clean up 'em flies when they start decomposin'? Look at that one."

They both go silent, and the room fills with loud breathing, likely the result of Lynell staring off with his mouth wide open. I don't understand how anyone would want these two dipshits working together. One's an asshole, and the other, despite looking a little more intelligent, doesn't know how to follow rules.

"Well?" snaps Goatee. "What'd ya see?"

Lynell clears his throat. "Um, I guess it looks like that one's starting to decompose."

His voice sounds more nasal than earlier, likely because of the stench in here. It doesn't bother me so much anymore, though. Breathing in the scent of decomposing flesh and internal organs all night seems to have desensitized me.

"Come on, help me out," says Goatee.

The two of them move toward me and the pile of dead bodies, and I focus on keeping my body limp as they pull on the bodies beneath me. The pile shifts, but only a bit. Our combined weight is enough to keep most of the bodies in place.

"Harder," grunts Goatee.

Something pops—assumedly a shoulder tearing out of its socket—and Lynell shrieks like a five-year-old boy.

"Quit being such a pussy," Goatee says. "Move."

Goatee grumbles something and tugs, shifting the pile one last time. A loud thump echoes throughout the room.

"See? Was that so fuckin' hard?" Goatee says.

Lynell clears his throat. "Well, I'm sure that all my tuggin' really helped—"

"Grab her feet and let's get out of here," Goatee cuts him off.

I peep through the crack of my eyelid as they drag a woman's body through the exit. The moment

they're gone, the door slams shut, and I'm alone
with a body I can't even use and a dying cricket in
my mouth.

CHAPTER 9

My eyelids flutter as I fight to stay awake. Through the window, the sun's blinding red light deepens to a crimson, before darkening to maroon.

"Yeah, I got it," comes a husky voice.

Who is that?

Closing my eyes, I focus all of my attention on the voices outside.

"Watch out for that one," Goatee says. "She's been a little witch all day. Haven't ya?"

The other voice doesn't respond, and Goatee continues complaining about every prisoner.

"And that one right there—"

"I've got this," says the husky voice.

Goatee mutters a few more words, no doubt leaning into Lynell like a gossipy school kid, before his voice fades. Where did he go? And who's the new guard? Was he here last night? It's difficult to remember anything with how messed up I've been.

I listen attentively. He doesn't make any noise for a while, until finally, he gets up from what sounds like a wooden stool, grabs something, and starts walking down a hallway. His footsteps fade in the distance, before reemerging on the right side of my door at last. Along with the sound of his footsteps, a tiger-orange glow creeps through the bottom crack of the door.

What's he doing? Patrolling?

Since I can't see him, I listen all night, until I realize that approximately every hour—3,600 seconds, to be precise—he gets up from his chair and patrols the entire floor with what I assume is a torch in his hand.

The next day goes about the same. I listen to everything I can, slowly learning the guards' schedule. Three hours after sunrise, Goatee and Lynell go out to feed the pigs and someone else comes in to watch the prison. The ground starts shaking eight hours later, and they go out again, I assume to meet Krusher and take whatever he has to offer them.

When they enter my room today, however, nobody is thrown over me, which means Krusher probably grabbed a pig. Either that, or they let him keep his catch.

"Can ya do it this time?" Goatee asks, a mocking laugh slipping in with his words. "Or do ya need help from a real man?"

I roll my eyes behind my lids.

Lynell remains quiet and the pile shifts until someone's head hits the cement. "This is real messed up. I don't get why Krusher can't eat 'em fresh. Why does he like 'em decomposing?" With one more tug, the pile moves and I tumble down, hitting my face square against a wall.

Goatee doesn't respond.

"So when are we getting rid of that little witch?" Lynell asks. "She's been bugging the crap outta me. If you ask me, she's a waste of supplies. We shouldn't even be feeding her."

"Well, I didn't ask you, Lynell," Goatee says. "And besides, you know the rules. We gotta keep her alive until the moon's full."

Lynell sighs. "And when's that again?"

"Two more nights," Goatee says.

"Well when that time comes," Lynell says, "I wanna be the one to bring her down to the lab. Her and the old hag." He grunts and a body drags against the cement floor.

Little witch? Old hag? Are they talking about Rachel and Zerachu? Who else could they be talking about? Rachel came into the castle looking for Zerachu, which means they're both in here, if they're still alive.

The guards drag the body out of the holding cell, going on and on about how much easier their jobs will be once those *two* are gone.

When the door slams shut, I instinctively ball a fist.

My hand.

Breathing out slowly, I attempt to open my hand, and to my surprise, all of my fingers extend.

I'm healing.

I try my other hand, and although difficult, I pry my fingers apart. I reach for my weapons belt. As expected, there isn't much of a belt left. Both of my Glocks are warped, as are my knives. With difficulty, I whip my wrists sideways and my blades come out, although one of them appears a bit crooked.

Nothing that can't be fixed. At least I still have them.

As the evening goes on, I count every minute until, as predicted, the night guard steps in to cover for Goatee and Lynell. He comes in two hours after sunset, and more specifically, one hour after Goatee yells at someone, telling them to go to sleep.

Like the night prior, the guard begins his patrolling and goes on to repeat this every hour on the dot.

The next morning, I manage to sit upright and stretch my arms, then my legs, until finally, I stand upright. Although thrilled that I'm regaining my mobility, one problem remains. Every time I move any longer than a minute, I feel depleted. If I don't feed soon to make up for this lost energy, I'll never make it out of here.

I position myself back against the ground before Lynell and Goatee enter the room again, looking to pick from the bottom of the pile. They bitch back and forth about how they can't wait to get rid of the witches, and it takes everything in me not to rip their throats out.

If I weren't so weak, I'd do it without a second thought. But I'm afraid that the moment I stand up to confront them, I'll fall back down. This has got to be one of the shittiest feelings in the world.

So instead, I wait.

The best plan of attack is to go after one guard, not two.

I stare at the cement ceiling as the sun sets and focus my energy on healing the rest of my body. One good meal. That's all I need, and I'll be back to normal in no time.

Finally, the time comes.

Goatee and Lynell switch with the night guard. Eventually, the night guard scrapes his chair out of the way, grabs his patrol torch, and heads off in the opposite direction.

I have one shot at this—if I don't act fast, I might collapse before making it out of here. It doesn't help that I'm going into this blind, but I don't have much of a choice.

The moment I no longer hear his footsteps, I spit Ace out of my mouth and place him at the far corner of the room.

He tumbles on his back, his legs pointing upward.

Fuck.

"Ace?"

He doesn't move.

"Ace?" I poke his belly, and one leg twitches.

He's barely alive. I need to move now.

Blowing out a lungful of air, I get up, my legs wobbly, and head for the door. Any other day, I'd open this thing as if it were nothing more than a flimsy piece of cardboard. But with how depleted I am, it's like trying to move aside a five-hundred-pound slab of cement.

After working at it, I pry the door away from the doorframe long enough to slip through the crack. Exhausted, I stumble out, catching myself against another cement wall. I glance up, seeing for the first time what I've visualized in my mind over the last several days.

As expected, it's a prison. Everything is made of cement—the floors, the walls, the window frames. The place looks to be centuries old. Barred windows run along the top edge of the right wall, and similar to my window, they're covered in iron bars. Next to them are lit sconces that cast a warm orange glow throughout the prison. Along the left side of the corridor is where the cells are. I'm too far down the corridor to see inside of them, but the big iron gates at the front of each one make it obvious they're prison cells.

Holding the wall to support me, I move forward, one unsteady step at a time, passing by snoring prisoners. All I need is an empty cell for my plan to work, but the problem is, they're all full. What the fuck am I supposed to do? Any minute now, the guard will reappear behind me, and it'll be game over.

While I could attempt to use my Lure on him if he catches me out here, he'll be on the offense, making it that much more difficult for my Lure to work. Trying to take someone's guard down requires even more energy. Energy that I don't have. I need to catch him while he's calm, which is why I wanted to get inside one of the cells.

From behind me comes the sound of approaching footsteps, and the guard's warm light creeps up the corner wall.

"Fuck it," I mutter, rushing toward the nearest cell.

It's too dark to see who's inside, but I'll take my chances. I'd rather be trapped with a prisoner than out in the open with one of the castle's guards.

Closing my eyes, I grab two of the prison bars and pry them apart as hard as I can. My face gets hot, and my temples throb, but the bars widen away from each other. I squeeze in sideways, pushing my breasts up and down to squeeze myself through the narrow opening. The second the guard's light spreads down the corridor, I squeeze the bars inward, bringing them back to their original position.

My head spins, and I hold on to the bars to stop myself from falling.

I feel so depleted, so nauseated. If I don't make this work, I'm fucked. I've used up the only bit of

energy I have left. If my plan doesn't work, no way
am I getting back out.

C̶HAPTER 10

"Get to bed, inmate," growls the guard.

His features, bumpy and rigid, look demonic behind the flickering glow of his torch and his brown skin as he moves closer to me.

"I-I'm sorry," I say, feeling like I'm going to pass out. "I had a vivid dream."

"If you don't get back to bed, I'll give you a nightmare," he says.

All I want to do is project my Lure onto him, but it isn't working. I'm too weak. So instead, I approach this differently. If I can't talk my way out of this, I'll have to get creative.

Smirking, I pinch the bottom of my shirt, pull it up over my head, and take it off.

"Back to bed!" he growls, his voice carrying throughout the prison.

"You're going to wake everyone," I say softly. "I can be quiet, if you want me to be."

He hesitates, his eyes darting from side to side.

I unclip my bra, then my jeans, and pull them down to my ankles, along with my panties.

"What're you doing?" he asks, his eyes flashing with hunger.

Without a word, I step toward the prison bars and press my bare breasts against them. It's cold against my skin, but I don't mind. Not if I'm going to get a meal out of this.

"No one has to know," I whisper.

With jittery hands, he reaches for a set of metallic keys on his belt and starts flipping through them like he downed three cups of coffee. When he finds the right one, he quickly unlocks the gate and steps inside. I'm still too weak to stand straight, so instead, I keep my hands wrapped around the bars, waiting for him.

Looking behind me, I say, "I'm all yours."

He smiles and enters the cell like he owns it and grabs me by the hips.

Then, he takes me.

It feels so fucking good that I don't want it to stop.

But when he eventually reaches his peak, I spin around, caress his face with the back of my hand, and pull my lips up to his.

His life force surges through me as if I've been injected with the world's most potent drug. It rushes through my lungs, my veins, my every cell, energizing me instantly. He stares into me as I drain him, his eyes slowly sinking in and his cheekbones becoming more and more prominent.

It's a sullen look that makes him resemble a

zombie.

The energy coursing through me is too invigorating for me to stop. I pull, and pull, until his face lightens, and uneven black lines zigzag across his skin.

His eyes, now empty of all life, stare at the concrete ceiling as I lower him to the ground.

I suck in a sharp breath through my nostrils and let it out through my mouth with a loud sigh. "Now that's what I'm fucking talking about."

Bending down, I pick up the guard's set of keys. It isn't until I stand back up that I hear it—someone grunting. I narrow my eyes and peer into the darkness of the cell, until slowly, the man's silhouette comes into view.

I can't make out any features, though he appears old with a rounded back and scrawny little arms. Is he...?

"Oh, for fuck sakes—" I start, but it's no use.

If the guy wants to jack off after watching two people go at it, he can do whatever the hell he wants.

With my new set of keys in hand, I slip back into my clothes and leave the cell. I reach for the nearest torch and yank it out of its sconce, then make my way at a gradual pace down the prison hall. As I pass each cell, I peek inside, looking for Rachel.

Some people are sleeping, others staring at me with big gumballs for eyes.

It isn't until I reach the fifth cell that I see her.

"Rachel?" I hiss.

She shoots upright as if waking from a nightmare and turns her head from side to side.

"Rachel, it's me," I whisper.

This time, she jolts off her bed and comes running to the gate.

She's clad in brown cotton prison rags that look like they were designed for a man twice her size. Her sleeves, both rolled up to her elbows, make her arms look like twigs. Both her feet are bare, and they're covered in dirt as if she was assigned the task of cleaning the pigpen every day.

I feel awful for her, but now isn't the time to exchange stories.

"What? How'd you find me?" she whispers sharply, no doubt wanting the prisoners to stay asleep as badly as I do. If they get rowdy, it'll only be a matter of time before another guard comes to investigate.

"It's a long story," I say, sorting through the dozens of keys. "I'll tell you about it later."

I try a couple, but none of them fit.

"It's that one," Rachel says, pointing to a key that looks like the rest of them.

I arch a brow and she smirks. "See that?" she says. "Number 11. That's my cell number."

"Of course it is," I say, feeling like an idiot.

The moment I turn the key, a loud clicking sound echoes throughout her cell and her gate opens with a whiney creak.

"Listen," I say, "I'll explain everything soon, but right now, I need your help."

She gives me a brief nod that I interpret as, *Anything.*

"Can you change people's shapes?"

She steps out of her cell, stretches her arms, and stares through the barred window and up at the starless sky. "What do you mean by shape?"

"Ace was turned into a cricket," I say matter-of-factly.

Her jaw goes slack and she plants two hands on her hips. "How'd you pull that one off?"

"It wasn't me," I say. "It was Jamieson."

Rachel stares at me blankly, as if Jamieson is supposed to mean something. I guess to her, it wouldn't. She doesn't know who he is or how I make my money. So instead of explaining the fact that I'm a hired hit woman, I flick a wrist. "Zane's dad, actually. I used to work for him. Turns out he was a warlock. But listen, that's not important—"

Her fists tighten into white-knuckled balls at the sound of Zane's name. I'm willing to bet he turned out to be a real asshole the moment they got here, but I don't pry. If she wants to talk about it later, I'll listen, but right now, Ace is all that matters.

"This is important, Rachel," I say, and her features soften. "He's going to die if we don't bring him back."

She cranes her neck, glances from side to side

down the prison corridor, and says, "There's one slight problem."

A slight problem is never a *slight* problem—everyone knows that. Whatever dilemma she's facing will have a tremendous impact on whether Ace gets to live.

Sighing, she says, "They took all my stuff."

Is this supposed to mean something to me? She's acting like she revealed some big secret.

"All my stuff," she says again, and this time flicks the air with an invisible wand.

"All your magic stuff," I say coldly.

She nods.

Great. Fucking fantastic. How is she supposed to bring Ace back if she can't even use magic?

"Can't you say a spell and point a finger at him?" I ask, my voice coming out snarkier than intended. It isn't her fault. But I'm freaking out. When I left Ace in the cell full of dead bodies, I knew there was a good chance I might be returning to a dead bug. Then, I found Rachel, and a spark of hope ignited within me.

"I wish I could," she says, "but I'm not *that* advanced yet. All I know how to do by heart is make a portal, and even then, I need ingredients. So I need my books, my powders, my wand. Especially my wand. It helps me focus—"

She stops talking when I pinch the bridge of my nose. I swallow hard, reminding myself that getting angry solves nothing. We need a solution, not a bitchfest.

"Where's your stuff?" I ask.

She bites her lip. Okay, so it's clear there's more to this than I thought.

"In some sort of sick magic testing lab," she says. "Zerachu's sister runs the place."

My stomach sinks. "Beatrix? How do you know this? And where's Zerachu? Did you find her?" I make my eyes pop out as I step from side to side, peering inside each cell next to Rachel.

"She told me," Rachel says. "Well, not in so many words. And that was before the guards separated us."

What the hell is she talking about?

"You know that game, where people have to guess what the other person is trying to say without using words? Well, it started out like that, and then—"

She's doing it again—blabbing away when all I need is a straight answer. She must sense my irritation; she clears her throat, twiddles her thumbs, and says, "Zerachu's in cell number eight."

Seriously? Why the fuck didn't she lead with that? If anyone's powerful enough to bring back Ace without a wand, it's the Great Witch. I storm down the corridor, scanning the iron room numbers at the top of each cell.

"It's no use!" Rachel shouts, chasing after me.

Voices erupt around us and hands appear through some of the prison bars.

"Hello?"

"Someone's out there."

"Hey, let us out of here!"

My heels tick as I move closer to cell number eight, fidgeting with my set of keys.

"No, Alexis, you don't understand—" Rachel says, but I don't listen.

I shove the key inside the lock hole, its scraping sound masking Rachel's voice, and tug hard on the gate until it opens with a screech.

Storming inside the pitch-black cell, I call out, "Zerachu? I know you're in here."

Something shifts at the far right corner, and out from the darkness comes a hunched figure. At first, I barely recognize her. She's lost so much weight that her cheekbones point out, making her look like a dying vampire... Hah. A dying vampire. Now that's an oxymoron. She moves toward me, one fragile step at a time, and leans the weight of her body against what looks like an old wooden staff.

"Zerachu?" I say.

She takes one more step toward me, and that's when I see it.

Her lips, torn to shreds, are stitched together by thick black thread.

"What the fuck happened?" I say.

Rachel comes jogging up behind me and stops cold in front of her great-aunt. "I tried to warn you," she says, her voice aimed at the floor. "They cut out her tongue and stitched her mouth up so she couldn't cast any spells."

CHAPTER 11

"He's in here?" Rachel says, hopping to keep up with my long strides.

Without responding, I march toward the cell of dead bodies and tell her to wait for me.

"Come on, let us out!" someone else shouts.

I return with Ace's cricket body in my hand and a sour feeling in my stomach. "This isn't good," I say.

From inside the nearest cell comes a woman's wet face, burgundy red eyes, and hairy knuckles. "You can't leave us in here to rot."

"Would you all shut up?" I snap, my voice bouncing off every wall in the prison. Surprisingly, no one talks back. "I'll get you all out when it's safe, okay? I need to focus on something right now and I can't have you all attracting new guards in here."

Again, no response, which is what I was going for.

"I'll give it my best shot," Rachel says. "I used this spell on Riskus when he fell and scraped his knee, and then on me when I stubbed my toe in here. I mean, it gave me a tattoo the first time around."

She goes to pull up her sleeve, but I grimace. "You're dealing with a cricket here, Rachel. You either get this, or you don't. And if you don't, you'll be killing him."

She gulps. "We don't have much of a choice. He looks like he's already dead."

The moment I drop him into her hands, he rolls around like a dry roasted peanut. She pokes at him and one of his antennas flicker.

"Well, he isn't," I say. "At least not yet."

When I realize I'm coming across like a bitch again, I soften my tone. "You can do this, Rachel. I know you can."

A spark flashes in her eyes—something I rarely have the pleasure of seeing. Is this the result of my encouragement? Do my words have that much impact on her? And then it hits me. Rachel's mother doesn't even know about her magic, which means she has no one to look to for positive reinforcement. The poor girl's been putting up with my constant criticism, and right when she thought she was about to get a world-renown mentor, it turned out to be the wrong great-aunt.

Zerachu could have done so much for this girl, and instead, Beatrix manipulated her into giving up some of the most powerful—and most dangerous—items out there. Her confidence must be shot.

She sucks in a deep breath, closes her eyes, and hovers a finger over the insect. As she breathes out, she speaks three words, all of which I don't understand, and then taps her finger on the cricket's belly. A green light spits out of her palm and shimmers across Ace's belly.

"Did it work?" I ask.

"I think so," Rachel says.

We wait, staring at the lifeless bug when suddenly, his legs twitch. Rachel's big, green, illuminated eyes shoot up at me and she grins from ear to ear. At the same time, Ace rolls over and lands on his legs.

I'm about to shriek with excitement, so instead, I pull Rachel into a tight hug. "Holy shit, kid, you actually—I mean, I knew you could. That was amaz—"

Rachel's elbow jabs me in the torso as she tries to pull away. "Um, cricket. I have a tiny helpless cricket here."

I jump back, wipe my hair out of my face, and clear my throat. "Oh, shit. Yeah. Sorry."

Rachel clears the awkward space between us with a shake of her head. "It's only a healing spell, so it'll help him for a bit, but I still need my stuff if you want me to try to change him back."

I refrain from commenting on how stupid of a statement that is. Of course, I want him back to his human form, for several reasons, one of them being that fine body of his. I must be making the face I make when I fantasize about sex. Rachel contorts her features like she's about to vomit and spins on her heels. "Are we going to the lab, or what?"

"What about us?" someone calls in out a mousy voice.

The prisoners. As much as I don't want to alert the guards, those prisoners might prove to be useful. What better way to sneak into some secret lab than to distract the guards with a bunch of rampant prisoners?

"Hold on," I call out to Rachel. She waits, arms crossed, as I pluck the first key from its ring. I'm about to start unlocking cell doors when the sound of rapid footsteps echoes nearby. It isn't coming from inside the prison.

"Back in your cell," I hiss at Rachel.

She darts, her bare feet slapping against the hard cement, and quietly shuts the gate behind her to make it look she's still locked inside. Up ahead, a thick wooden door bursts open. I expand my wings, propelling myself up toward the ceiling.

I land with my wings sprawled out and my wing claws dug into wooden support beams.

"I didn't hear anything, Lynell. You sure you ain't smokin' some stuff again?"

Lynell shakes his head, which from up here, looks like a bird's nest. A bald patch decorates the top, and around it is messy, wiry hair that forms a doughnut.

"Something isn't right," he says. "I heard people talking—"

"What'd ya mean, you *heard*? You're supposed

to be on break, Lynell. It ain't our shift."

"I know that," Lynell hisses back. He tears a torch off the wall and holds it up in front of his face. "I was standin' outside when I heard some voices coming through that window." He points at the window under me, and I hang above in silence, feeling like a total ninja.

Slowly, Lynell leads the way with Goatee behind him—a sight that doesn't look natural.

"Where's Tyson?" Goatee says, his bug eyes darting from side to side.

I assume Tyson was the night guard's name. You know, the one I fucked and sucked dry. In time, they'll find his body. Or, shit. The gate. I never closed it. That also means the creepy man I caught jacking off might be wandering the prison halls.

Lynell raises his torch even higher, and that's when it happens.

A loud chirp.

"Is that a fucking cricket?" Goatee says, moving his chin around like he's trying to cut the air with it. "Where'd that come from?"

Ace chirps again and I roll my eyes. He's either feeling great now that Rachel healed him, or he's doing it on purpose. Who knows how that man thinks, even when he's a bug.

"Right there," Goatee says, brushing past Lynell. "Hey, you!"

Rachel steps out from within the darkness. "Oh, hey. What's up, guys?"

Both Goatee and Lynell exchange a look that could translate to, *Who is this girl and what has she done with the witch?*

"What's that noise you're makin'?" Goatee asks.

"What noise?" Rachel asks, her tone smug and fearless.

Arrogance suits her. She reminds me of a younger version of me. I like it.

"What you got there, ya little witch?" Goatee barks. This time, he leans forward and grabs the iron bars with his fists. The moment he leans his weight against it, however, the door shifts and he stumbles forward. "What the fuck?"

With bulging biceps, he tears the door open. "How the fuck did this happen?"

Rachel shrugs. "How should I know? Must have been the wind."

Goatee breathes out hard like he's about to blow a fuse. With rounded shoulders and balled fists, he takes a step inside her cell, as does Lynell. "Think you're real smart, don't ya? Beatrix might want your magic, but accidents happen all the time. Like you slippin' and smashin' that pretty little skull of yours."

With no emotion whatsoever, Rachel steps toward them, and both men instinctively lean backward. "You know, just 'cause I don't have my wand, doesn't mean I can't turn you both into frogs."

I, for one, know she's bluffing, but these two

twits don't know that. Goatee clears his throat like he's trying to swallow his fear. "You ain't that powerful, sweetheart. Ain't nobody gonna protect you in here."

"Oh, that's my cue," I say aloud, and both their heads snap back toward me. I drop from the ceiling and fold my wings, sending a gust of wind so powerful toward them that they both stumble backward with flailing arms.

"What the f—" Goatee says as two curved horns come tearing out of his forehead.

If he thinks morphing into his demon self is going to protect him, he's an idiot. Wait, I already knew that. His nose elongates, as does his chin, but that's all he has time to do. With a strong flap of my wings, I propel myself into Rachel's cell, grabbing the two twits by their throats. Rachel ducks right in time as I fly over her with both men at my sides, the tips of their toes dragging on the ground.

I don't land.

Instead, I aim their heads at the wall with my arms out in front of me. The impact is fast, hard, and satisfying. Both their skulls split, and a colorless slime oozes out onto my hands. In an instant, I let go, dropping their bodies to the floor, and shake off whatever nasty shit came out of their heads.

With my head held high, I step out of the darkness. "I like them better when they don't talk."

Chapter 12

Taking the time to let out the prisoners is a risk, but how can I not do it? They didn't ask to be kept here. And I'm willing to bet they don't deserve it, either. Whoever's running this place must be a sick, sadistic piece of work.

Is it Beatrix? Maybe. It would make sense, after all. From what I understand, she's sucking magic out of people. What for? Well, for the same reason any evil villain does what they do—to gain more power. I don't waste time trying to understand the mind of a psychopath. All I give a shit about is getting Ace and Drax back, and then, if I'm up to it, saving the world.

We'll see how I feel.

Rachel makes her way down the prison's corridors, opening each cell as she goes. Prisoners come running out, their grins stretching their filthy faces as if they've won the lottery. If I weren't so preoccupied with my mission, I'd be curious about how long each prisoner's been held captive.

"Do you know where the lab is?" I ask Zerachu.

Without a word, she nods.

"Listen," I say, pointing a finger at the stitches over her lips, "we'll get that fixed, okay? Hell, if magic can turn my friend into a cricket, it sure as hell can fix your face."

She glowers at me.

"Your stitches. Not your *face*."

At least she still has her messed-up sense of humor.

Then, I hesitate. "Can't you point at yourself and make magic?"

This may be a stupid question—if it *were* possible, she'd have done it already. To my surprise, she nods but uses weird hand gestures that make no sense to me. She points at herself and waits.

"You," I say.

Another nod, followed by her pointing toward the ground.

"Listen, lady, I've never been good at playing games with people." I smirk, fighting the urge to make an inappropriate joke. "We could go at this for hours and I still wouldn't know what the fuck you're talking about."

Her eyelids go flat and she shrugs as if to say, *Your loss.*

Zerachu isn't the type to be offended by bluntness—she's like me in that way. If there's one thing she hates as much as me, it's people beating around the bush. I won't sit here nodding politely as she tries to explain something to me that I know for a fact I won't understand.

Neither one of us has time for that shit.

Finally, Rachel comes back, her cheeks rosy and a slight pant in her breath. "All done."

"Thanks, Rachel," I say, getting up off of Zerachu's prison cot. "Zerachu says—" Again, I smirk and glance sideways at the Great Witch. What the fuck is wrong with me? I have too much energy and it's spilling out all over the place. "Well, she *tried* to explain—"

Rachel rolls her eyes. "I get it. She can't talk. Spit it out already."

"She can lead us to the lab," I say. "And maybe you'll know this. Why can't she magically remove her stitches? You can't tell me you witches *always* have to blurt out some verbal spell."

"We don't," Rachel says, "but they did something to her. I don't know what. Her magic doesn't work."

"Well, isn't that fucking awesome," I say. Sighing, I crane my neck and stare up at the ceiling. "The whole point of coming to rescue the Great Witch was so she could help us stop the war."

I realize I'm being insensitive when I sense Zerachu's flaming gaze on me.

"No offense," I say, "but it's not like we're family. I wouldn't have come looking for you unless—"

Rachel's spiteful glare catches me off guard.

"Oh, right," I say, remembering they're related. I flick a wrist in the air as if we're discussing something as trivial as the ingredients found in crayons. "Well, we need to fix her. If you get your magic stuff back, you think you can help?"

My last words are aimed at Rachel, and she knows it. She may not be as powerful as Zerachu, but she has her blood. Maybe Zerachu can guide her in fixing whatever they did to her.

"I can try," Rachel says.

"Good," I say. "Now, come on, let's get down to that lab and get this over with."

I'm about to walk out of Rachel's open prison gate when Zerachu steps in front of me. What the heck is she doing? She may not be able to talk with those horrid stitches over her lips, but she doesn't have to. Her face says it all.

"Okay, what is it?" I say.

With arms crossed over her chest, she jabs a finger at the ground and gives me her famous stern look—the one most people use to describe the woman, which is *Angry Russian Lady*. With brows knit close together, she jabs the air again and makes animated hand gestures that make no sense to me.

Yet Rachel appears to be absorbing every little detail. She nods slowly, her chin inside her palm, then nods again. "Yeah, she has a point."

Is she for real? How on Earth can anyone understand this woman's self-taught sign language? It's like watching some drunk play Pictionary.

Hesitant, I wiggle a finger at Rachel, then at

Zerachu. "You can't possibly have understood—"

"She says we can't barge into Beatrix's lab. It's too dangerous. Her sister is powerful and we have no idea what we're walking into."

I'm too confused to say anything, so I tighten my lips.

"We have to come up with a plan," Rachel says.

A plan. That's a great idea. There's one problem though. Planning takes time and effort—two things we're short on.

Impatiently, I throw my arms in the air. "Well? You got something, or not? Because if you don't, I'm going down there and killing her myself if I have to."

Zerachu takes a step toward me with a stiff finger in my face. Rachel doesn't need to translate this one for me. She still cares about her sister regardless of what's going on, which means killing her is out of the question.

"All right, I won't kill her," I say, sighing louder than necessary. "Doesn't mean I can't hurt her."

Zerachu's fierce glare warns me that if anything happens to her sister, there will be consequences.

How does that make any sense? She has an evil twin sister threatening our entire world, yet she chooses to defend her. Am I missing something? I thought evil family members got disowned. Although tempted to explain to Zerachu that Beatrix could be the cause of an apocalypse, I don't. What's the use? Blood is blood. And if Zerachu is still trying to protect her sister after what she's done, well, then no amount of words will change how she feels about her.

"I don't think you understand," Rachel says, shoulders drawn back. "You might be strong and powerful, Alexis, but you can't fight magic, which means you can't face her head-on. Beatrix could turn you into a bowl of steaming soup if she wanted. Look at what happened to Ace. It took all of what, one second? We need to be strategic about this."

The kid's right, which pisses me off. But I'm also happy to be fighting alongside a smart witch like her. At least now I know she isn't a liability.

"So what do you propose?" I ask. "It sounds to me like we need a distraction, but we're running out of—"

Someone shrieks, and the sound of swords clashing against each other echoes throughout the castle halls.

"Catch them!" comes a guard's commanding voice.

Dozens of footsteps stampede down in one direction, shaking the castle walls. War cries erupt throughout the corridor, followed by the sound of weapons and fists bashing against bodies.

Smirking, Rachel turns to me. "Wasn't what I had in mind when I released the prisoners, but that'll work."

Chapter 13

The air feels cool and damp, as if we've ventured fifty feet below ground. But that isn't the case. We've descended two flights of old cobblestone stairs. If I didn't know we were making our way to a lab, I'd think we were descending into a torture chamber.

Hell, for all I know, the lab serves that purpose, too. We are going into an evil witch's lab, after all. As we move deeper into the firelit corridor with cobwebs dangling overhead, I'm relieved to have left Ace behind. He's safe, for now. I left him inside a small hole in the cement wall of Rachel's cell.

With a rounded posture and crazy hair, Zerachu scurries down the castle corridor, turning her head back every few seconds to make sure we're following. I keep scanning the ground, expecting to see rats running around. I hope to the gods that I don't see any. They're such a distraction with their cute whiskers, their beady little eyes, and their humanlike hands that make you want to feed them.

Zerachu stops cold in her tracks and Rachel

bumps into her. The skin around her stitches stretches as she tries to form words, but nothing comes out. With bulging eyes, she points a thick-jointed finger around the corner. Again with the nonsense.

I'm about to say, *For fuck's sake, woman, if you're going to sign, at least do it properly*, when Rachel nods briskly and turns toward me. "Did you get that?"

I give her my *Are you kidding me?* look and open my mouth to release my thoughts, but she cuts me off before I can. "Beatrix is in there. We have to wait."

"Wait for what?" I whisper.

"For her to get—" Rachel says, but suddenly, heavy footsteps echo in the distance.

I close my eyes and listen, trying to tune out the sound of Zerachu's heavy breathing.

"I-I don't know," says one of the guards.

Another male.

Don't they have female guards around here? There are two explanations for this, both of which are sexist: someone created this place with the ideology that women are too good to be guards, or the complete opposite—women aren't capable of being guards.

"You have to come with me."

"Get your hands off me!"

That voice. It sounds like Zerachu's. She must have read my mind. She turns around, a sour expression on her face, and for the first time I understand what she's saying: *That's my sister.*

"Are you a fool?" comes a voice similar to Zerachu's. "Tonight is the night! I can't possibly leave now. I have too much to prepare."

Beatrix.

"The prisoners are running wild. It isn't safe," the guard says.

Beatrix lets out a hoarse scoff. "Oh, for cryin' out loud. Do I have to do everyzhing myself?"

Heels click and the sound of shuffling carries throughout the basement. "Go! Out of my way!" she says. Though I can't see her, it's easy to imagine a witch with the same mannerisms as Zerachu—hands sweeping the air like those of a mother shooing kids out of the kitchen.

When the shuffling softens, Zerachu turns around and wiggles her finger, telling us to follow. She leads us around the corner, down a narrow hall, and through a series of sticky spider webs. I dodge the biggest by bending back as if preparing to do the limbo and walk face-first into a smaller web filled with dead flies.

In a panic, I lick my hands, desperately trying to get all that nasty shit out of my mouth without making a sound. I must look like a total moron. When Rachel senses me waving my hands all over the place, she gives me an uneven-eyed look that says, *What the hell is wrong with you?*

Why couldn't we have encountered rats? Why

spiders? Chills run down my arms as I shimmy past a huge black widow with curled legs.

We head through a narrow opening built of old rotting wood and enter a room that can only be described as chaos. Clear glass jars filled with colorful potions clutter a maple counter, and around them are textbooks with watermarked and bubbled pages. Several broken wands lay about sporadically, along with powders and bits and pieces of materials I'd prefer not to question.

My attention is instantly pulled to high-pitched squealing and whining at the far back. The moment I turn, I'm filled with both despair and rage. There are dozens upon dozens of cages lined up against the back stone wall, and inside are creatures of different shapes and sizes. Some look like dogs, others like cats, and some are impossible to make out. It's as if Beatrix has been experimenting by swapping genes from one creature to another. One dog, in particular, sits up the moment I look at him. He tilts his head, scratches his ear with his back paw, and starts panting with a wide doggy grin.

"Are you fuck—" I start, marching straight toward the cages.

Zerachu's icy grip on my wrist stops me in my tracks. The woman's stronger than I expected, and the firmness in her grasp is enough to shake me out of my anger.

"She says we'll help them after," Rachel says.

I squint an eye. "Okay, what is it with you two?

Did you learn a secret language while you were locked up?"

Rachel, who seems taken aback, crosses her arms and leans the weight of her body onto her heels. "What? No. I understand—" But she stops and scratches her head. A huge grin splits her face. "Holy crap. I think I can read minds."

Zerachu rolls her eyes, points at her arm and wiggles her finger between herself and Rachel as if pointing out an invisible line connecting the two of them.

Surprisingly, I understood that one. "I think you can read *her* mind."

Beaming, Rachel paces around the room and the animals shift excitedly in their cages with every step she takes.

"How's that even possible?" Rachel starts. "I mean, I'm a witch. But mind reading? That's something totally different. So, like, if I think of something, you can hear my thoughts?" She pauses as Zerachu shakes her head. "Oh. Okay. It has to be intentional. So—" She goes quiet, glares at her great-aunt, and waits.

Reluctantly, Zerachu raises one arm and scratches her armpit.

What the fuck is happening here?

Rachel lets out a laugh so loud all the animals bark, chirp, and squeal in response. "It works!"

"That was your test? You asked her to scratch her armpit?" I say, unimpressed.

"Well, she can't talk," Rachel says. "Had to be something random."

She's about to send Zerachu another mental message when I step between the two of them. "Listen, I'm happy for you and this weird little thing you have going with your great-aunt, but we don't have all day here. Find your shit so we can go save Ace and Drax."

Rachel sighs as if I asked her to clean her room, then moves around the laboratory to find her things. Zerachu does the same, gliding her fingers across glass jars and old parchment paper.

As I inspect the lab, I can't help but wonder—was Beatrix seriously going to drain a bunch of innocent people of their magic? And her sister, at that? What could have led her to be so evil? Zerachu, for the most part, turned out to be a saint. Okay, that's an overstatement. She's a bit of a bitch, but the woman has a good heart. She believes in kindness—again, for the most part—and would never harm anyone on purpose. Okay, unless they *really* deserve it. There's a reason she was assigned the role of watching over the Dark Hall. People admire and trust her, regardless of how crude she can come off at times.

It makes no sense to me that someone of that bloodline—Rachel's bloodline—could be so cruel. Then again, plenty of families have a black sheep child. Even serial killers have siblings that wouldn't hurt a fly. I've always believed that such an anomaly has to do with a bad soul being injected into a body.

Beatrix has either always had a dark heart, or her evilness is the result of years of pain.

If the latter is true, it still shouldn't justify capturing her own sister and intending to suck out all of her magic.

"Aha!" Rachel shouts. My shoulders jerk forward and my hand knocks a jar off the countertop. It shatters next to my feet and I release my wings, propelling myself into the air.

There's no telling what the slimy shit will do if it touches me.

Bad idea.

The gust my wings create sends several other glass jars whirling through the air and crashing against the stone wall.

"Alexis!" Rachel cries out. With her mouth agape, she faces me with a wand in one hand and a book of spells in the other.

Retracting my wings in an instant, I wince as a way of apologizing. "That shit could have turned me into mush!"

Without any expression, Zerachu bends forward, dips her finger into the gooey substance, and raises it to her nose. She flicks it off, stands back up, and nods at Rachel.

"Yep," Rachel says. "Turns fae into fertilizer for the pigs."

My jaw drops. "Are you fucking kidding me?"

Zerachu shoots me a nasty glare. I don't think

she appreciates it when I swear. She's pretty old-school, which means cursing around younglings is something she doesn't condone. What she doesn't seem to realize is that we're living in the twenty-first century. Eight-year-olds swear, for crying out loud. Rachel will soon be an adult.

A sly smirk curves the corner of Rachel's lips.

"You little sh—" but I stop myself.

"Come on," Rachel says. "That was funny. And for the record, it's *lopsera*."

"What the hell's that?" I ask.

"An ingredient," Rachel says as if discussing pasta sauce. "It's a staple for potions. Can come out all sorts of different colors, but it's safe. Doesn't do anything unless you mix it in with other ingredients. Kinda like butter. You wouldn't eat that on its own, right? But with it, you can make so—"

I make my eyelids go flat and Rachel seals her lips. I'm all for having a good conversation, but more often than not, Rachel doesn't know when to stop talking, and when that happens, the words that come out of her mouth are irrelevant or unimportant. It's like she needs to emphasize her point over and over again with the use of an analogy *and* a metaphor. I'm willing to bet if I didn't cut her off all the time, she'd offer to write me a step-by-step guide explaining everything in detail.

I'm about to tell her that her prank wasn't as funny as she thinks it was when loud footsteps enter the laboratory.

"Well, well, well," comes a purring voice.

I spin around so fast my expanded wing slaps Rachel across the face. She grimaces and swats at it as if trying to shoo away a stubborn horse fly. Thankfully, it wasn't my claw that hit her.

At the entrance of the laboratory stands a spitting image of Zerachu. Well, with more meat on her bones. Aside from that, the only difference between the two is their attire—Zerachu's covered in gray prison clothing, while Beatrix stands proudly with a purple frilly dress that looks like something out of a Halloween costume shop. Her long hair, blond and scraggly, sits over one shoulder the way Zerachu wears hers.

Tilting her head, she smiles at us from behind piercing green eyes and seems amused by either our boldness or our stupidity.

"And here I thought I'd never see you two again, what with the prisoners escaping and all." Her eyes linger on me for a moment. "And who are you?"

Before I can answer, Rachel steps in front of me and plants her hands on her hips. "She's with us, and if you so much as try—"

Beatrix clicks her fingers and Rachel bursts into a cloud of pink smoke.

I'm about to lunge straight for Beatrix's throat when Zerachu does it for me. Beatrix, looking unbothered, sighs and clicks her fingers again as the tips of Zerachu's fingers graze her neck.

Zerachu disappears instantly, but before I can react, Rachel's whiny voice echoes from above.

"You can't do this!"

Above me, Rachel kicks back and forth from within the confinement of a black, oversized birdcage. Her legs dangle through the bars, and with fingers wrapped around them, she shakes as hard as she can, causing the entire cage to sway back and forth. "Let me out of here, you old hag!"

Zerachu finds herself in the same predicament next to Rachel, only instead of heckling Beatrix, she's giving Rachel the stink-eye. I assume this might have something to do with calling her *twin sister* an *old hag*.

Beatrix swirls a finger in the air and Rachel's cage starts spinning in circles. She then lets out a loud cackle and does the same thing to her sister.

"Would you stop that?" I say, fists clenched.

I'm not in any position to fight a witch, especially one with her level of mastery. I may be strong and immortal, but I'm not an idiot—even I know my limits. The fact that she fooled the entire Dark Hall into believing she was Zerachu makes her someone to be wary of, and if I'm not careful, she might click her fingers at me. Unlike Rachel and Zerachu, who happen to be her family, I may not end up in a birdcage.

Beatrix stops twirling her finger, reaches for a spell book, and spins back around before I can ask her what she's doing.

"Quite ironic that the two of you would come straight to me," she says, flipping through the pages of her spell book."

If I were to close my eyes, I could easily mistake Beatrix for Zerachu. Her voice is identical, well, aside from the accent. Unlike her sister, Beatrix sounds like she was born and raised in America.

I take a step forward, but immediately regret doing so. Without raising her head, she looks at me from her peripheral, her pointed nose appearing twice its length from this angle. "I wouldn't try anything stupid, sweetheart."

Sweetheart? Now she's pushing her luck.

Then, as if realizing something all of a sudden, she slams her book shut in her hands and raises her head. "Are you the one who released the prisoners?"

Is this a trick question? Does my fate depend solely on the answer I'm about to give?

Instead of responding, I force a smile and do the unthinkable. "I have to say, Beatrix, you look much younger than I imagined."

A hint of a smirk pulls at the corner of her lips as I project my Lure onto her. I'm about to throw another compliment her way when she swats the air and grimaces. "A succubus! I should have known." Pacing, she grabs at her long hair over her shoulder and plays with it almost compulsively. "I haven't thought about another woman like that since 1942."

Rolling her eyes, she shakes her hands the way one does after washing their hands, only to find out the paper towel roll is empty. What the fuck is she doing? Shaking off my Lure? Is that even a thing?

"Beatrix, darling." I take another step.

"Nope!" she shouts. "I won't have it! The last time I ventured into the world of lesbianism, I lost five years of my life!"

What the fuck?

Slowly, I glance up at Rachel and Zerachu, both of whom shrug at me. My stare lingers on Rachel. I planned on telling her what kind of demon I was at some point, but I guess it's too late for that now. In retrospect, telling her I had sex with my victims would have been a lot better than her watching me trying to seduce an old woman.

Surprisingly, though, she doesn't seem at all bothered. She throws her chin out as if to say, *Keep doing whatever it is you're doing.*

Beatrix's pacing gets faster and more sporadic as she moves around the laboratory in search of something. "I will not give in to your... poison."

"Poison?" I say, smiling seductively her way.

Hips swaying, I move toward her, sliding my fingers along the wooden countertop. When my finger catches something slimy, I wince and pull away.

"I'd hardly call my desire a poison," I say, inching closer toward her.

With her back facing me, she scavenges

through an old chest, throwing all sorts of tools and artifacts over her head.

"Aha!" she shouts, pulling out a dusty bottle full of neon yellow liquid.

She pops off the cork, slurps it back, and places the empty bottle back into its rightful place.

Fuck this. I'm running out of time. With my claws extracted, I bend my knees and jump straight for the back of her scraggly head. Suddenly, I find myself sitting in my very own birdcage next to Rachel.

"Damn it," I mutter.

Below us, the witch clears her throat and lets out an awkward laugh. "That was too close for comfort. Thank the goddesses I had my anti-lesbian potion on me."

I cock a brow. Is this witch for real? "I'm sorry, did you just say anti-lesbian potion?"

She glowers up at me but doesn't respond.

"Aren't you aware that we're living in the twenty-first century? I think it's time to step out of the closet."

She stares at me, confused.

"All I'm saying is, the fact that you need a potion at all—"

"Shut your trap, you filthy demon whore!"

Smirking, I keep my mouth shut.

"What are you?" she asks, her eyes narrowing into slits. "I've met many succubi in my lifetime, but you—you're something different." She rubs at her chin as her eyes glaze over. "Something powerful."

Fuck. Does she sense that I'm a demigod? Can she suck that out of me the way she intends to drain Rachel and Zerachu of their magic?

"Sorry," I say. "I don't know what you're talking about."

An ugly grin stretches across her wrinkled face. "That's it. That's the answer. I may not have the other prisoners, but you—" She points a crooked finger at me, her arm trembling. "You'll suffice."

Chapter 14

"Aren't you two supposed to be sisters?" I say.

Beatrix ignores me and instead stirs her cauldron full of floating bits and particles. One item, in particular, looks like someone's big toe. It's enough to make me want to vomit in my mouth. She mumbles a bunch of nonsense, no doubt preparing her spells, and throws a pinch of powder into her mix.

What the hell was that? Dried organ?

The liquid erupts, creating an electric cloud full of bright yellow zaps. Then, as quickly as it erupted, it disappears back into the cauldron.

"Well, I can see where she gets her manners," Rachel says. "Rude. Exactly like her sister."

Zerachu moans through her stitches, reaches through the bars, and claws at the air, trying to catch one of Rachel's hanging limbs.

"See? And they're both crazy," she adds.

I give Rachel the stink-eye. What the hell is she doing? Why is she trying to provoke *both* of them?

"Oh, quit wastin' your breath," Beatrix says.

"Getting Zerachu angry won't combat the spell I put on her."

"Spell?" Rachel asks, inching closer toward the bars. "What spell?"

Beatrix turns her face to the side just enough for Rachel to see her smiling. "You didn't honestly think I'd stitch her mouth and call it a day, did you? So long as Zerachu stands within the castle, her magic is useless. My goddesses, child. Who raised you?"

Rachel looks at me for a moment, as if wanting my advice on how best to handle Beatrix. But before I can even open my mouth, she squeezes her cage's bars, presses her face against them, and says, "Your sister."

Beatrix scoffs. "Zerachu doesn't care for children, and she sure as hell didn't waste a moment of her long miserable life raising one."

"I wasn't talking about Zerachu," Rachel says.

Beatrix's fist solidifies around the handle of her ladle until the thing snaps in half. She turns around and points the sharp broken wood at Rachel. "What did you say?"

"I'm talking about my grandmother, Celeste."

Beatrix scoffs, trying to fluff off Rachel as if she were nothing more than a toddler rambling on about some fictitious story. But when Rachel hardens her features, Beatrix shifts her gaze toward Zerachu. "Is this true?"

Zerachu stares coldly at her sister without

responding.

"Oh, for Zeus's sake." Beatrix sighs, points a finger at Zerachu, and says, "*Expidere.*"

At once, the stitches on Zerachu's face vanish and she opens her mouth repeatedly, stretching her jaw. "You sneaky little—"

I guess she got her tongue back, too.

Beatrix jabs her broken ladle upward, her pointy knuckles whitening. "Don't you start mouthing off, you wench. I took off your stitches and gave you back your tongue but I can sure shut you up again!" Saliva sprinkles out of her mouth and she stabs the air, her long blond hair slipping off her shoulder and falling behind her back.

Zerachu takes in a deep breath, closes her eyes, and says, "Zhe kid isn't lying. She's your great-niece."

Beatrix looks like she wants to scoff again, but it's obvious she's more taken aback than anything. With one hand on her hip and the other still holding the sharp piece of wood, she switches her focus from Zerachu to Rachel, and then back to Zerachu.

"Why are you doing this, Beatrix? If Celeste could see what you've become—"

"Don't you talk about big sis!" Beatrix snaps. "You have no right. You're both pig shit cowards, you know that? Lockin' me up for twenty years." Her eyes narrow into dark slits. "I'll never forgive you. Ever! You deserve whatever's comin' to ya!"

"Vhat zhe hell are you talking about?" Zerachu

says. "Who told you zhis? No one locked you up."

Beatrix whips the air with her hand and this time, an iron slab bolts itself over Zerachu's mouth. She moans out in pain and claws at it, but it's no use.

"That's better," Beatrix says. "And as for you two"—she grabs a new ladle, sticks it into her cauldron, and points at us without looking back, droplets of potion dripping next to her feet—"I suggest you learn from what happened and keep your damn mouths shut."

I do as I'm told and sit for what feels like hours as Beatrix goes on rummaging through boxes, cupboards, and drawers in search of books and ingredients. Whatever she's concocting, it's complex. I suppose it would have to be if she intends to suck all the power out of us.

How the fuck am I supposed to get out of this one? I can't use my Lure. That stupid potion of hers made her immune. I can't use brute force. She'll turn me into a puddle of Jell-O before I even reach her.

Think, Alexis, think.

Beatrix shrieks with excitement, shaking me out of my trance. With a hunched back, she leans over her black cauldron, scoops up a spoonful of bright green slime, and sniffs it.

"Perfection!"

Zerachu slaps her forehead and then presses it against the cold iron bars.

Does she really not know why Beatrix is doing this? I mean, shouldn't sisters know this stuff? She can read minds, can't she? If so, her sister's behavior shouldn't come as a surprise. That's what evil siblings do, right? Evil shit.

Rachel glances over at Zerachu, nods, then shakes her head.

Great. They're having a telepathic conversation that I can't be a part of. Whatever they're planning, it had better be good, because the first person Beatrix is going to dispose of is me, the nonwitch.

Zerachu gets animated seeing as nothing is coming out of her sealed mouth, until finally, Rachel spins around to face me and whispers, "She says Beatrix isn't being herself. She's never had a mean bone in her body, so Zerachu thinks this is some type of spell. She tried to talk to her telepathically, but it isn't working."

"Can it be broken?" I whisper back.

Rachel shrugs. "Zerachu has no idea what's going on."

I clear my throat and Beatrix's shoulders tense up at the sound. Knowing it's a risk, I part my lips, prepared to smooth-talk my way out of this, when loud footsteps come stomping into the laboratory.

At first, I assume it's a measly castle guard, but the moment I see his face, my fists tighten so hard around my cage's bars they bend.

"You son of a bitch!" I shout.

Rachel glowers at me. She's no doubt as angry

as I am to be looking at Zane's fugly mug, but she appears to have better control over her emotions than I do.

Zane looks up nonchalantly and smirks, his arrogance making me want to break out of this cage and throw him through one of the castle walls.

"Would you look at this," he says. "I'm surprised to see you here, demon." He steps toward Beatrix, towering over her short body. "What the hell is going on, here, witch? You were asked to do a simple task. My father doesn't want demons. He wants witches. How fucking clear do we have to be about that?"

Beatrix's knuckles whiten around her ladle again, but she doesn't talk back to him.

What the fuck is going on? Why would a powerful witch like Beatrix be kneeling before some kid warlock?

"My father will be here at midnight," Zane continues. "I expect that winged creature to be disposed of before then."

"You don't understand," Beatrix says.

At once, Zane raises his arm and backhands her across the face.

Zerachu screams from behind the metallic plate over her mouth and punches the air.

"You're a coward, just like your father," I say.

Again with my big mouth. I'm locked in a cage, and if Zane has learned anything from Jamieson, he's learned some pretty powerful magic.

Zane's features soften and he straightens his posture. Cupping his hands together, he says, "On second thought, keep her alive. My father will be pleased to find out she's been captured."

Not knowing what to say, I flip him the bird as he walks out of the laboratory.

Fucking jackass.

The second he's gone, the room fills with an eerie silence. Both Zerachu and Rachel look upset by what happened, but no one's willing to speak up. So, being that I'm the one with the big mouth, I do what I'm best at.

"Hey, Bee."

She snaps her head sideways, that long nose of hers making an appearance again.

"He shouldn't have treated you like that," I say as kindly as I can.

"Don't pretend to care!" she hisses.

"Listen," I say, "I get it now. You're working for Jamieson. Guess what? I used to work for him too."

This seems to capture her interest. She turns a little more and looks at me with one eye.

"He's a bad man, Beatrix. You can't trust him."

She remains quiet, which leads me to believe I'm making progress.

"He's also a warlock, and if I were to guess, I'd say he implanted false memories in your mind."

"Liar!" she snaps. "I was beaten and tortured for twenty years because of her!" She breathes hard through bared teeth, her eyes so large it looks like they're about to burst out.

Zerachu clenches a fist outside of her cage.

"She says that's not true," Rachel says. "She visited you last year, don't you remember?"

"What kind of trickery is this?" Beatrix says, moving toward the cages. She cranes her neck to look up at Zerachu and Rachel.

"In the woods, next to Pinkora Lake," Rachel adds.

Beatrix gasps, her hand hovering over her open mouth. "Pinkora Lake," she mumbles. "But that can't be. No, that's not possible! I don't know what you're talking about. I haven't been to Pinkora Lake in decades!"

Rachel shakes her head. "That's not true. Zerachu says you only found out about Pinkora Lake after my grandmother—your sister—died, and you had a cabin built to seclude yourself."

"Enough!" Beatrix shouts. This time, Rachel's the one to receive an iron slab over her mouth.

She whimpers the moment it makes contact and frowns with her eyes crossed.

"Beatrix," I say, raising my hands in submission. "I won't to try to talk you out of anything, okay? You want our powers? They're yours."

With her face as red as a tomato, she waves her arms over her head. "I don't *want* your powers, you stupid, filthy demon! I have no choice!"

"Jamieson's going to use his magic to hurt a lot of people. Is that what you want?"

She doesn't respond.

"All right, what's Jamieson paying you? I'll double it, okay? Let's stop this now."

She sucks in a sharp breath and glares up at me. "Your money is useless to me. Jamieson released me from my prison in exchange for my soul. Once I do what he's asked of me, I'll get it back. And I'm the only one powerful enough to take Zerachu's magic, which means no one else can do this but me. Now shut your damn mouth. I have four hours left before midnight."

And with that, she throws her magic at me and an iron slab smashes me in the mouth.

Chapter 15

Use my super strength.

Don't use my super strength.

Use my super strength.

I balloon my cheeks and press them up against the cold bars of my cage. I stand a chance, right? I mean, Beatrix is so preoccupied with perfecting her last potion that she hasn't looked up at us in over an hour. The way I see it is that I have a better chance of surviving Beatrix than I do Beatrix, Zane, and Jamieson combined. Once the ritual starts tonight, I'll be surrounded by so much magic that the idea of escaping will be nothing more than a fantasy.

Fuck it.

It's now or never.

Sucking in a long breath, I pry the bars apart as hard as I can. But the moment they stretch away from each other, they snap right back into place.

What the fuck?

Without looking up at me, Beatrix lets out an evil chuckle. "I guess they're right about beauty and brains not being friends.”

With my mouth covered in metal, I glare down at her.

“It’s encased in magic, you foolish demon.”

Great. Of course it is. Now there’s no way out of this.

Rachel and I exchange a look, and I slant my eyebrows apologetically. I can’t help but feel like this is all my fault. I should have never let her come here on her own, and worse, I shouldn’t have stolen the book from her. What was I thinking? Now, this innocent witch will be stripped of her magic and maybe killed because of my selfish ways.

Feeling like a complete moron, I avert my gaze, but Rachel draws my attention again when she clears her throat. She shakes her head at me, and although no words come out of her sealed mouth, the softness in her eyes tells me she doesn’t blame me for anything.

Why is she being so nice about this? I try to smile, but all this does is hurt. Instead, I lean back into my cage and close my eyes. Maybe if I fall asleep, I’ll miss out on the whole ritual.

When someone comes walking into Beatrix’s laboratory, I awake. The sound of the person’s footsteps are slow, calculated, and soft. Behind me, the caged animals start freaking out.

“Looks like you have everything under control, my dear Beatrix.”

I snap my eyes open to find Jamieson standing

tall next to the evil witch. Raising his scruffy, salt-and-pepper chin, his gaze turns on me, and a malicious smile creeps onto his face.

"Well, isn't this interesting," he says, his British accent no longer sounding sexy.

He folds his hands together the same way Zane did a few hours ago, tilts his head, and says, "And what do you intend to do with this one, Beatrix?"

Beatrix rushes to his side like an abused troll—arched back, short steps, and a hand positioned next to her face as if preparing to block a blow. It's sad to see her this way. Her bloodline is powerful and has always fought against injustice. To see her obey Jamieson like a slave obeying some cruel master is both sickening and disheartening.

"She's powerful, this one. There's something about her," she tells him.

Jamieson's bright, penetrating eyes narrow on me. "There most certainly is."

The words come out as if he knows about my family lineage, but how could he? No one but Ace knows that. He stands on the heels of his shiny leather shoes. "Is everything prepared, Beatrix? The moon is in position."

She nods rapidly, rushes to her table, and uses her new ladle to scoop out a sample of her potion. With a single glance its way, Jamieson smiles. "It looks fantastic."

Beatrix smiles back, though it's obvious she's only hoping he'll be pleased enough to give her back her soul. The moment Jamieson bends forward to look at it, Beatrix shoots her sister a look—one of uncertainty and fear.

Are her memories returning? Or, is her bond to her sister that powerful? Right now, Beatrix is the one person who can get us out of here.

"All right, let us begin," Jamieson says.

Beatrix's eyes enlarge and dart up at her sister again.

Jamieson, perhaps sensing her doubt, leans the upper half of his body to lower himself to her level. "Must I remind you that your sister is the one who imprisoned you all those years? The one who decided which form of torture should be used on you?"

Zerachu shakes her cage wildly and moans behind her slab of metal.

"She is a monster, Beatrix, and the sooner we get this over with, the sooner you can go on living the life that was stolen from you."

As if suddenly reliving her horrific years of made-up imprisonment, Beatrix frowns up at Zerachu and spins her body to face the cauldron, her long purple dress following her movement.

Fuck.

I'd give anything to tear Jamieson's face off with my claws. He watches me arrogantly—a look that shouts, *I win*—and I can't help but feel like he might be right.

I'm the one sitting in a fucking giant birdcage

with no way out.

Beatrix turns back around with a bowl in one hand and her ladle in the other. A fine mist spills from the top of the liquid and licks at her fingers, her wrist, and her forearm.

The three of us start shouting from behind our metal mouth plates. Rachel kicks her legs so hard that her cage bumps into mine. I'm tempted to tear off my mouth plate and tell them both to rot in hell, but it's infused with magic, which means my strength doesn't stand a chance against it. And for all I know, it'll tear my face off.

Surprisingly, Jamieson doesn't put a stop to our freak-out. It's like he's reveling in it, and the more we panic, the happier he becomes. The second I grasp this, I stop jerking my cage around, and instead, stare him cold in the eyes.

That motherfucker will pay for this one way or another, even if I have to come back in spirit form and haunt his ass for all of eternity.

As Beatrix scoops her potion and drops a giant glob under each one of our cages, I experience something I haven't felt in centuries—fear. I've come close to death many times, but having my powers stripped from me? This is a first. If Beatrix succeeds, there's a good chance she'll suck my immortality right out of me, which could kill me in seconds. If I'm suddenly human, that'll make me one thousand years old and I'll explode into a pile of dust.

I swallow hard, and just as everyone describes in the movies, my life starts to flash before my eyes—vivid memories of everything I've done, every person I've ever met, and every city I've explored. Then, I think of Veerka and hope to the gods she's okay. How can this be happening? I was supposed to make it back to her. My feelings for Veerka shift over to Ace, and my stomach fills with painful nausea.

He's going to die, too. He's a goddamn cricket, lying helpless inside a concrete wall.

And what about Drax? Oh, fuck. Drax. Is he okay? The nausea makes me gag behind the metal plate as Mr. Mushroom's big brown eyes and wagging butt pop into my head.

Please take good care of him, Riskus.

The pile of green gunk underneath us starts to sizzle, and Beatrix whips out her wand, along with the Heart of Danu.

Jamieson reaches for it and slips it over his head and around his neck. The heart-shaped gem glows a crimson red in a pulsating pattern like a beating heart. The red glow illuminates his face, accentuating his evil features along with his malevolent grin.

With her wrinkled, veiny hand, Beatrix raises her wand toward the ceiling, aiming its tip at each of us one by one.

Clasping the talisman, Jamieson's focus shifts to me. "Start with her."

My heartbeat quickens, and for the first time in my life, I feel cornered. There's no way out of this one.

Beatrix closes her eyes and starts reciting some verse in Latin. With her wand aimed at me, she jabs it into the air and shouts, "*Expelious!*"

A boltlike flash zips out of her wand and comes straight for me, hitting me in the chest. Had I not seen the magic coming my way, I'd have presumed I was impaled. I've been shot at more times than I can count in my lifetime—guns, arrows, you name it. But this pain doesn't compare to any of my past wounds. It's a hot, searing pain that makes me want to die instantly.

Beside me, Rachel stares at me with eyes so big and watery I hardly recognize her. I try not to mimic her expression, but the pain is so excruciating—even more so than being crushed by that cyclops—that I can't even bring myself to pretend otherwise.

After the pain comes a sensation of depletion so pronounced that my head rocks back and forth.

The talisman around Jamieson's neck lights up a fiery red, and he grabs it as if trying to touch the power with his bare hands.

I want to shout. I want to find a way out of this, or even better, wake up and realize it was all a dream. But that doesn't happen. Instead, I look over at Rachel one last time to let her know how sorry I am for everything I've done.

She tries to shout, her cheeks red and puffy, but nothing comes out.

And then, everything goes black.

CHAPTER 16

"Alexis."

Is... is someone calling my name? If so, this means I can still hear, which indicates I'm still alive.

Great. Fucking fantastic. Why am I still alive? I'm useless without my powers. I'd have preferred death over becoming a lowly feeble. I'm afraid to crack my eyes open, but when the familiar voice echoes beside me again, I can't help but peer through the crack of my eyelid.

In front of my face is Zerachu's big nose. She winces, scratches her head, and breathes out hard through her open mouth, releasing a century-old stench.

"Dude," I say, turning away from her poisonous stench. I'm so weak that the idea of standing up nauseates me. "What's going on? Where am I?" I raise my hand and extract my claws. Three of them come out, but that's all I need to know I haven't lost all of my powers.

"It vould have been nice to know you had a friend like zhis," she says, ignoring my question.

"We thought he was a cricket," comes Rachel's voice.

Rachel!

I manage to force myself into an upright position. She's sitting next to Zerachu, her back against a bale of hay inside the pigpen.

"Rachel, what's going on?"

She looks both happy and horrified. Rather than responding to my question, she jerks her head sideways in the direction of the pigs. I crane my neck, hoping to catch a glimpse of something, but I can't see anything other than pink and brown pigskin everywhere.

"I don't have the energy for this. What am I looking at?"

She arches both eyebrows and with her nose, points in the same direction again. This time, I spot a limb—a very familiar limb with a Battalion ring wrapped around its middle finger. I want to jump to my feet, but I don't have the strength.

"Ace—" My voice cuts out, so I clear it. "Ace!"

Although his name comes out louder, it sounds hoarse and raw.

"How... how is this possible? We're alive?"

Rachel nods. "Thanks to that guy."

A cool shadow looms over me. I spot slipper-like shoes, and hanging over them is a forest green cloak with gold stitching. That cloak. I've seen it before. I manage to lean back a bit more to look my new savior in the face, but I'm greeted by a hooded figure.

"You," I say.

Slowly, he reaches for his hood and removes it to reveal dark brown skin and piercing green eyes. His brows, black and unkempt, suit his rugged look. Across his plush pink lips and down his chin runs a pink scar—something that appears to have been caused by a claw. He rubs at his clean-shaven face and gives me a look that translates to *Nice to see you again.*

Nice isn't the term I'd use. This guy, who I first thought was a warlock, recently shot fireballs at me in Adam Shaw's basement.

"You torched my ass," I say.

He smirks, making it difficult to hold onto my resentment. "My apologies."

Despite my resentment, his deep voice soothes me.

When I don't say anything, he adds, "I do hope you will accept my act of kindness as a way of making things up to you. You know, for the trouble I have caused. I also meant to thank you for your brave efforts."

What's he talking about? I'm happy to accept an apology, but what is he thanking me for after all the shit I've caused? And what act of kindness is he talking about?

I'm about to question him further regarding this *act of kindness* when he tilts his head toward Ace, and everything makes sense.

"You turned him back," I say.

"And took zhis crap off of us." Zerachu points at her mouth, referring to the metal her sister used to shut us up.

"Ace got us all out of there," I mumble.

The dark-skinned man clasps his hands in front of his belly, his long, oversized sleeves merging together. "You granted me my freedom."

"You were imprisoned?" I ask.

He nods. "Before you released everyone from the castle, I overheard you speaking about this friend of yours, Ace. I thought you may be in need of his assistance. After all, the Battalion must fight together." He pulls his arm out of his sleeve, revealing a shiny Battalion ring.

So he wasn't a bad guy after all. When he found me in Adam Shaw's basement, he must have thought I was after the *Book of Origin* and the Heart of Danu for all the wrong reasons. How could he not? I'm a demon, not a witch, and I didn't have a Battalion ring at the time.

He stiffens his stance, allowing his sleeve to fall back down. "Your friend appears to be in rough shape. He said you could help him with that. I don't suppose you know what he meant?"

I know exactly what Ace meant, but the problem is I have no energy left to share with him. If I plan on giving Ace a little boost, I need to be entirely replenished myself. Standing right in front of me is my best option, but draining this witch of his energy, even if I don't kill him, isn't a very good idea—the guy saved our asses, and he also happens to be part of the Battalion. With everything going on, we need as many soldiers as possible.

"What's your name?" I ask.

Smiling politely, he says, "Fabian."

I'm about to introduce myself when he releases a soft chuckle. "And you are Alexis."

"How—"

"This Ace gentleman only said it about a hundred times or so."

If I weren't so weak, I'd smile. Instead, I close my eyes and sigh. "I have three witches around me right now. Can't one of you heal him?"

Zerachu shakes her head before Rachel manages to get a word in. "His veakness stems from his demon biology razher zhan a vound or illness. I can't fix zhat vith magic. I've already tried. All I managed to do vas give him a little boost, zhe way Rachel did inside zhe castle."

If Drax were here, he'd come up with some idea so stupid it would be worth considering.

"Rachel," I say, snapping my head sideways. "Didn't you say these pigs are people?"

She bites her lip and looks over at the pigs. "Um, yeah. That's what Zane told me."

"That means Drax might have made it through the portal," I say, more to myself than anyone else. "Listen—"

Something shifts from within a pile of hay

nearby and I stop talking. Although too depleted to put up a fight, I clench my fists nonetheless.

"It's her, I know it," comes a familiar voice.

"No, it isn't safe."

"Get out there."

"Stop it."

The pile of hay dances from side to side as the bickering continues.

"Relax, guys," I say, matter-of-factly. "It's me, Alexis. Get out here. It's safe."

Safe might not be the best way to describe our current predicament. We still aren't sure how we plan on getting out of here, and it won't be long before Jamieson and Beatrix find us.

Out from the muddy hay comes the three captives I met in the pigpen when I first arrived at the Kingdom of Shadows—the young man, the older southern gentleman, and the kind Asian woman.

"You came back," says the young man.

I want to nod and tell them I wouldn't have left them behind, but in all honesty, this was a fluke. If it weren't for Ace, we'd all be dead, which means the three of them would have been crushed by the cyclops.

"Who—" Rachel starts, but I raise a trembling hand.

"Don't worry about it," I say. "They're friends."

After a prolonged silence, I say, "We don't have much time, so I need all of you to listen to me very carefully. Can you do that?"

Everyone nods.

I swallow hard, a lump sliding down my throat. "Zerachu, I need you to work on a portal capable of letting through as many people as there are pigs in here."

Rachel's jaw drops as if I asked her great-aunt to construct a three-mile bridge using a hammer and a bag of nails, but Zerachu nods, seemingly unbothered by the simple request.

"Fabian, Rachel, I need you to turn these pigs back into people. And you three—" I wiggle a weak finger in their general direction. "As soon as people start reappearing, guide them toward the portal, okay? No one stays behind."

Rachel crinkles her nose at me. "And what do you plan on doing?"

I gaze out toward the castle where an ominous cloud hovers above its towers. "I'll make sure everyone makes it through safely."

Rachel opens her mouth to protest, but Zerachu wraps an arm around her shoulders.

When no one moves, I click my fingers. "*Andale,* let's go."

I don't have to tell Zerachu twice. Without the use of a wand or powder, she makes gestures with her hands and shouts, "*Itinerantur, ahk dalous!*"

I understand the first Latin word—Travel—but the rest is pure gibberish. Well, at least to me, and I know over a dozen languages.

She flicks her fingers as if trying to sprinkle water in someone's face, and out through her fingernails come electrical flashes of blue and neon yellow light. They spit, zap, and spark as they blend to form a giant spiraling portal.

A few nearby pigs squeal as a powerful blast comes sweeping out of the large opening.

"That'll work," I say, staring at something that looks like ten of Rachel's portals combined.

Rachel's big green eyes remain fixated on Zerachu as if pleading with her great-aunt to show her some tricks. The Great Witch smiles—something I've rarely had the pleasure of seeing—and kisses Rachel on the forehead. "I vill teach you all I know, little one."

I stumble forward when a pig brushes against me and squeals.

"What's wrong with that thing?" I ask.

Fabian gives me a look, and I realize that *thing* may not have been the most appropriate of terms. All of these pigs are people, or at least, were.

Fabian raises a mahogany wand and says, "It's afraid, that's all. Wouldn't you be?"

"If I had some random witch trying to throw magic at me?" I say. "Gee, I don't know. I've never had that happen before."

Without so much as blinking, he flicks his wand at the pig and it bursts into a cloud of purple smoke. The smoke dissipates instantly, revealing a scrawny naked man with a thick brown mustache and squinting eyes.

"Wh-wh-what's going on here?" he says, cupping himself.

He pushes his finger up the bridge of his nose as if trying to readjust invisible glasses. "Oh, gosh darn it."

My cheeks balloon and I turn away before coming across as rude.

"What's so funny?" Rachel whispers.

"It's Ned Flanders," I say, my eyes watering.

She stares at me like I'm half her age.

"Oh, come on. If Drax were here," I try.

"Oh, man," comes Drax's voice. He stumbles toward us with a dazed look on his face and scratches the top of his scaly head. "What the hell?"

"Drax!" I shout, prepared to throw my arms around him.

Given that his man bits are hanging in the wind, I decide otherwise.

"Holy shit," he says. "Who brought Ned Flanders?"

I let out an exaggerated laugh in Rachel's face, and in an instant, I feel half her age, not unlike the way she looked at me seconds ago. Awkwardly, I clear my throat and straighten up.

"What happened?" Drax moans.

"You were turned into a pig," I say, "along with everyone else."

One by one, people begin to take on their human forms, and the crowd of pigs shrinks.

"Come on, come on, let's go!" shout my three pigpen mates. They rush around everyone, shooing them toward the portal as if trying to direct a herd of sheep.

"You too, Drax," I say, pointing my nose at the portal.

He grimaces. "What? No way. I'll go when you do."

Drax might be a super nice guy, but he's stubborn as hell. If he refuses to leave my side, there isn't much I can do short of throwing him into the portal, and I'm not exactly in the mood to grovel for his forgiveness for the next two weeks. Plus, I don't have the strength to do it.

"Fine," I say. "Then help me toss Ace into the portal."

If I weren't so weak, I wouldn't need his help—I'm stronger than a dozen Draxs combined.

He grins a set of incisors like he's prepared to fight a war, but then spins in a circle.

Pinching my eyebrow, I point at the shelter.

"Oh, right," Drax says, running to find Ace.

I'm amazed by how fast the crowd is clearing. The pigs are gone, and naked men and women hurry to the exit.

I'm about to ask if anyone spotted Marge Simpson yet when a deep rumbling tickles the bottom of my feet. I'd recognize that sound—that feeling—anywhere.

I shift my focus toward the castle and my

stomach sinks.

I'm not the only one who sees it. Behind me, shrieks fill the air, and panicked footsteps splatter through the mud.

Out from behind the castle comes the cyclops, his massive eye searching the sky. His attention is corrected the moment a dozen guards yank on the massive chain around his neck. A few of them dangle on the chain, holding on for dear life.

What the hell are they thinking trying to control something so big?

Surprisingly, it isn't the cyclops that scares me, nor the army of over a hundred soldiers in rank. What makes me sick to my stomach is the sight of Jamieson leading the cavalry. Next to him are Beatrix and Zane. In other words, even more dark magic.

"Um, guys," I say. "You might wanna move faster."

Bodies begin tumbling atop one another as people push their way toward the portal.

Drax appears next to me, his reptilian eyes narrowed on Jamieson. "You think we'll make it out in time? The dude looks pretty angry."

A blinding thunderclap illuminates the red sky, and black clouds begin to roll in.

"Yep," Drax says. "I think it's safe to say you pissed him off."

I give him my *You think?* look and he stops talking.

"Is Ace safe?" I ask.

He nods.

After a beat, Drax breathes out through his slits for nostrils. "You think we can take them on?"

I give him another look—this time, one that says, *Do you honestly want to know the answer to that?*

I may be strong and immortal, but I'm no match against magic. At least, not this level of magic. How the hell can I fight against Jamieson, Beatrix, and Zane? Oh, I almost forgot. And his entire fucking army? Including a cyclops? I couldn't even stand up to Beatrix in her laboratory. With a click of her fingers, she hung me inside a birdcage.

And that was after I'd fed.

Now, I'm weak and depleted.

We're royally fucked.

"I'll take that as a no," Drax says.

"Doesn't matter," I say. "Ain't no shame in running away. Let's go."

I spin around to find a few people remaining, including Rachel and Zerachu.

"Rachel, get inside, now," I order.

"Not until—" she tries.

"Get in the fucking portal or I'll throw you in myself," I snap.

I don't mean to be so cold, but there's no time to argue. I need to make sure that kid is safe above all else.

Another flinch-worthy thunderclap explodes

above our heads, and water drops from the sky as if being dumped by Dolos in buckets. And in case you aren't familiar with Dolos, he's the god of trickery and guile—and a conniving one at that.

"Go!" I shout, water splashing out of my mouth.

Rachel rushes toward the portal but slips in the mud. Behind her, Zerachu scoops her up by the arm and looks back at me one last time. We exchange a look, something beyond words. It feels like a reassurance. At that moment, I know that if something happens to me, Zerachu will take care of Rachel as if she were her own.

I offer Zerachu a nod of gratitude, and at once, she and Rachel throw themselves inside the swirling portal.

Three more people run through, clearing the area.

"Come on!" I shout to Drax.

I'm about to jump in when I spot something moving from my peripheral. Farther back is a brown-skinned teenage boy with huge, panicked eyes. He runs in one spot like a dog on hardwood flooring, mud splashing behind him as his legs kick out.

"Oh, Alexis," comes Jamieson's voice.

Although much closer to us, he isn't close enough to talk to me—especially in this heavy downpour. His voice sounds deep and heavy, almost demonic. When he speaks again, the sound comes from the clouds.

"There's no use running anymore," he says.

"Drax, go!" I snap, running to the young boy.

The second I reach him, I grab him by the back of the neck with one hand and with all of the energy I can muster, I throw him straight into the portal, his kicking legs inches away from Drax's face. I'm about to scold Drax for not having jumped through when another thunderclap explodes over our heads and a blinding lightning bolt tears through the clouds. It hits the ground this time and makes a loud snapping sound, like that of a tree being split in half.

There's one problem though: no trees nearby.

I see the terrified look on Drax's face before I understand what happened.

Behind him is a vast, wet field that resembles a pool of blood beneath the red sky. I wouldn't typically pay much attention to the scenery in a dire time like this, but the fact that I can see it at all is what has my stomach in knots.

"The portal's gone," I breathe, my words barely leaving my mouth as rain continues to pour.

Chapter 17

"Um, Alexis," Drax shouts.

I hear him, but I'm too lost in my mind to respond.

"It's quite rude to leave without saying goodbye," Jamieson says, his voice carrying through the sky.

How did I ever find his accent a turn-on? Okay—it was. But at the moment, I'm fantasizing about tearing out his voice box.

The ground beneath my feet trembles as the cyclops moves closer.

"If you have a plan," Drax says.

"I don't have a fucking plan," I snap.

I don't mean to take my panic out on Drax, and that's what I love about the guy—he knows that. He doesn't take my rage issues personally. Well, control issues. I have no control over anything at the moment, and it's eating me from the inside out.

I crane my neck and gaze up at the sky. As big black puffs roll overtop one another, I can't help but wonder—is this place even real? Or, are we in a magical dome somewhere out in buttfuck nowhere?

Anything is possible.

For a moment, I consider flying up as high as I can and attempting to tear through the overhead ceiling. But what if there isn't a ceiling? What if we're on some other planet? Then I'd be leaving Drax alone to die. Besides, with the little strength I have, I may not land without crashing into the Earth and breaking every bone in my body.

I'm screwed.

And not in a good way.

"Can't you charm your way out of this?" Drax says.

If Jamieson weren't, well, Jamieson, then maybe. But the guy knows what I am. No way will I be able to throw my Lure at him.

"How about we run?" Drax says.

With every step Jamieson and his army take, Drax's eyes appear to grow bigger.

"Anytime now, Alexis. Anytime," he adds, as if I have some secret plan to get us out alive.

When I don't answer him, his breathing quickens, and two gills open up on either side of his neck, flapping with every panicked breath.

"What the fuck?" I say. "Since when—"

"Focus!" he growls, his gills opening even wider. "Can't you just, like, I don't know. Fly us out of here? Jesus, Alexis. You're standing there like a goddamn statue. Do something about this or I swear to the gods—"

"The gods," I mutter.

"Are you high?" he snaps, his voice jumping up an octave.

"Surrender now, and I might be merciful," Jamieson shouts.

This time, his voice isn't blasted down on us from above. He stands several yards away, a smug look on his face. With a click of his fingers, the rain subsides.

"Oh, I do apologize if my lightning interfered with your escape."

Right. Like it was an accident.

He clasps his hands together in front of his belly and sighs like he's about to announce that his patience is thinning. I've grown so accustomed to seeing Jamieson in fancy suits that it takes my brain a few seconds to recognize him.

Around his body is a long black cloak with unusual designs printed in gold. It resembles an eye—similar to the evil eye—but its iris is bloodred and its lashes mimic Egyptian-style makeup.

I've never seen that design before, and it's not until my eyes roll toward his army that I realize it's engraved on the chest plates of every soldier.

Jamieson rubs the blond scruff on his face and removes his oversized hood, allowing it to sit neatly on his shoulders. That's when I notice the talisman around his neck—the Heart of Danu.

Son of a bitch.

"It's unfortunate it's come to this," he says. "Let me ask you one last time. Surrender now—"

"Eros," I mumble under my breath.

"What was that?" he asks.

I wasn't talking to him, so I don't bother repeating. If Ace is right and I'm part goddess, wouldn't that make me more powerful than everyone here? It may be wishful thinking, but I'm about to get killed. I have to try something.

Eros, if you can hear me, help me out here. You're supposed to be my dad, right? You ditched me for a thousand years. I'd say it's the least you could—

I cut my thoughts short. Apparently, I'm still holding on to some resentment. Let's try this again.

Sorry about that.

I pause, trying to gather only positive thoughts.

Jamieson says something, but I don't hear him.

Eros, Alice, anyone. Help me out. I'm asking for your guidance. I've never done this before. But here I am, asking for help. Please.

Suddenly, a faint, almost inaudible voice slips into my ear. "*Your power extends far beyond physical touch.*"

Holy shit. It worked. Someone's actually looking out for me. But what does this mean? I already know my Lure can be cast at a distance. How is seducing someone going to help me against an entire army of Jamieson's men?

Something hard hits me in the ribs and I'm jerked back to reality. Next to me, Drax makes his eyes pop out and clenches his jaw as if to say, *What the fuck are you doing?*

"I'll take your silence as an answer," Jamieson says. "I'm terribly sorry things had to end this way, Alexis. You were my favorite."

He clicks his silver-ringed fingers and turns around. Beside him, Zane smirks, looking about as evil as his father. What I wouldn't do to shove a hammer down that kid's throat. And her. My eyes move to Beatrix. Although a spitting image of her sister, I barely see the resemblance anymore. The two are nothing alike. This hag is an evil witch who deserves to be burned at the stake.

Wow, Alexis. That was pretty insensitive, even for you.

I don't give a flying fuck. If she were anything like Zerachu, she'd be putting a stop to this. She's powerful enough, yet she stands there, averting her gaze. She may not be relishing this, but it's apparent she's too much of a coward to do anything about it.

Behind the three of them, hundreds of armed men wait for Jamieson's command.

"Hey, Jamieson," I blurt out.

He turns his head enough to look at me.

"Eat shit," I say, throwing a handful of pig crap at his mouth.

It splashes over his lips and up his nostrils. He blinks several times, likely astonished that I'd have the balls to do something like. After a few seconds, he wipes it off with his cloak and bares his partially brown teeth at me.

Next to him, Zane takes a step forward, but his father stops him.

"That was a mistake, Alexis."

Stiffening his back, he stares at his army and shouts, "Kill them."

Without warning, Beatrix stomps on his foot and charges my way.

Jamieson spins around so fast his cloak whips through the air. "You fool!" he shouts.

"For Zerachu," Beatrix says, offering me a wrinkled fist. She aims her hateful glare at Jamieson, prepared to cast a spell on him.

"Cut them all to pieces," Jamieson shouts, "and start with the limbs!"

The second his army moves forward, an unusual tingling spreads throughout my fingertips.

Rage? Survival instinct?

Your power extends far beyond physical touch, I hear in my mind.

Suddenly, my wings blast out of my back and my horns tear out of my skull. Although weak moments ago, I'm more energized than I've ever felt. It's as if I had a secret energy store deep inside me—a store waiting for the right moment to reveal itself.

No way am I going out like this.

The sound of metal against metal fills the sky as soldiers extract swords from their sheaths. They move toward me, their large helmets casting

154

shadows over their featureless faces.

"You want a piece of me?" I shout.

Damn, that was the perfect time to use that phrase.

The second they charge forward, I extend my arms on either side of me and smile. I can't explain it, but the confidence I feel is surreal. It's as if nothing in the world can stop me—not even this army.

Collecting all of my energy, I narrow my eyes and throw my Lure at the first row of soldiers, moving from left to right. Their movements slow, hindering those behind them. With my mind, I open their mouths and suck in hard as I would when kissing my prey.

That's when it happens.

Something I never imagined possible.

Out from their dozens of mouths comes my favorite purple mist. It twirls through the air in thin lines like narrow ravines flowing through a secluded forest and into a lake. I part my lips as the mist moves closer to me, and the moment I taste it, I suck in hard, feeling a euphoria like no other.

One by one, soldiers drop to their knees as I suck them dry, their eyes glazed and their faces covered in black squiggly lines. I drain them entirely, and for the first time in my life, I feel like my true self.

Farther back, Jamieson stares at me as if witnessing a resurrection.

That's precisely how I feel, like I've been resurrected.

The second row of soldiers hesitates, some stopping midrun.

"Attack!" Jamieson shouts, his voice on the verge of breaking.

Try me.

An indescribable power courses through my veins, begging for release. It's as if this amount of power was designed for the gods, and being that I'm a demigod, I can only contain it for a short period.

Releasing loud battle cries, the soldiers point their swords at the sky and charge straight toward me. The cyclops, no doubt having been prodded by the men, charges straight ahead, too.

But it doesn't matter.

They won't survive this.

Although I have no idea what I'm doing, it feels natural. It's as if I've done this a thousand times before. I gather all of my energy and push it to the tips of my fingers, the initial tingling sensation amounting to a painful burn.

Jamieson must anticipate what's about to happen. In a flash, he and his son disappear, leaving behind nothing more than dancing green flames.

Shouting, I throw my hands out at the army, willing my energy to escape. It does exactly as I intend, and out from the tips of my fingers comes the same purple mist I sucked in mere seconds ago.

A powerful blast sweeps across the army, flattening them instantly.

The moment the blinding purple light fades, all that remains is a field of ash.

"Holy mother of Hades," Drax says.

Beatrix stares ahead without blinking. When she catches me staring at her, she swallows hard. "Holy shit, am I ever glad I switched sides before that happened."

"I bet you are," I say begrudgingly.

Why couldn't the woman have helped us sooner? Not that it matters. She did this willingly when she thought we were going to be killed. That speaks volumes. I think deep down, I'm still annoyed that she held me captive in a birdcage for hours.

I slap my hands together. "That was fucking kick-ass."

Mouths agape, neither of them says a word.

Chapter 18

What the hell is going on?

At the center of Lucky Cheetah Motel's parking lot, Zerachu and Beatrix stare intently at each other as if on the verge of playing a game of quick draw. With slouched shoulders and legs parted slightly, it won't be long before one of them takes the other one out.

Though I can't imagine either of those two witches firing a gun, maybe they'll play their version with an icy spell.

All that's missing now is some Wild Wild West theme music.

An empty soda can rolls across the damaged pavement as the wind blows through the crowd, its tin sound catching everyone's attention.

"Is anyone gonna step in, or...?" someone tries.

"Shut up!" comes another voice. "That evil witch caused all of this. Let the good one handle it."

Throughout the entire parking lot stands an audience that would easily fill up a movie theatre. Out from the torn motel come new observers, curious to watch the drama about to unfold.

Thankfully, all of the ex-pigs now have clothes, so I don't have to stand next to sagging or dangling parts.

Zerachu lets out a grunt and everyone gasps.

It's the first noise she's made in over an hour. Unlike most people here, I know exactly what those two witches are doing—they're talking shit out.

Rachel throws her arms in the air. "Screw this, I can't stand around and watch—"

I scowl at her. "Mouth."

She offers me a crooked smirk. "For your information, I'm seventeen as of today. You can stop trying to be my mother."

"What? It's your birthday?" I say.

She shrugs. "Yep."

I'm about to say something like *Oh, shit, well Happy Birthday*, when both Zerachu and Beatrix appear next to us. The sisters lean in, their long crooked noses reaching Rachel's shoulders.

"What?" Rachel says. "How was I supposed to know that?"

She pauses.

What the hell are they talking about now?

"Wait, are you serious?" she continues. "Or are you two messing with me?"

"What are they talking about?" someone nearby hisses.

I feel their frustration. It's annoying to listen to one side of a conversation. I have to try to fill in the blanks and imagine what those two witches might be telling her telepathically. Whatever it is, it's enough to get her excited.

Rachel beams. "Yeah. Yeah, of course I accept! Are you freaking kidding me?"

I stomp my foot between the three of them. "Accept what? You two witches can't come here and—"

Still grinning from ear to ear, Rachel says, "Turns out being seventeen officially makes me an adult in the world of witches, which means I can join a coven. Their coven."

"You two don't even have—" I start.

"Ve do now," Zerachu says, a rare smile on her thin lips. "The Power of Three is unstoppable. Ve had it vith Celeste years ago until she turned away from magic."

"The power of three," I repeat. Zerachu isn't wrong. Everyone knows about the power of three. The concept represents the triquetra symbol. By combining magic from three witches, the power is greatly intensified. And when combining it from three blood relatives, well, you can imagine. "You do know that Rachel doesn't have any formal training, right?"

"Not yet," Zerachu says.

What's that supposed to mean? She says that like she has any say in the kid's future.

She sort of does, Alexis.

I remind myself that I'm not Rachel's guardian.

We're friends—nothing more. I may feel the need to protect her, but I'm not her mother, and I'm certainly not the one who is going to be making decisions about her future.

That's up to her, her mom, and the Great Witches.

"We'll make sure she's ready for what is to come," Beatrix adds.

"So you guys are a team now?" I say.

Zerachu's eyes dart to her sister. "My sister was misguided."

Her twin averts her gaze, no doubt ashamed at what she did. "I'm sorry, sister, I should never have believed that asshole."

By asshole, she means Jamieson. The guy's pretty persuasive, especially when magic's involved. I don't blame the woman for believing the lies he implanted in her head. He *wanted* her to hate Zerachu, and that's what happened. He also made her believe he stole her soul, when obviously, he didn't. That isn't easy to do. Maybe for Hades, but not a warlock.

"All right," I say, "so what now? What's your big plan?"

Zerachu rubs her pointed chin, lost in thought. "First, ve speak vith zhe Elders. Ve must explain to zhem zhat zhe vampires did not do zhis and stop zhe var."

That sentence sounded like a fly buzzing in my ear.

"How do we know?" someone shouts. "What if this Jamieson guy was working for the vampires?"

I hold in a scoff. "Trust me, I know Jamieson, and he hates anyone who isn't him or his son. Especially vampires. What did he call them?" I tap my chin, trying to remember what he told me when he confessed to his ingenious master plan. "Brainless shells with sharp little teeth."

Gasps fill the cloudy sky and Beatrix nods. "It vas Jamieson and his son. He told me everything. Zhe vampires do not know about zhis. Zhey tink it vas zhe fae who cause all of zhis."

"Perfect plan, isn't it?" I say. "He wants both sides to destroy themselves so he can take over."

"So what do we do?" Ace asks.

His face no longer looks as green as Drax's, which means he fed off someone while I was fighting for my life against Jamieson. Involuntarily, my eyes narrow as I search the parking lot.

I wonder who it was. Realizing I'm being petty—jealousy doesn't look good on me—I push my thoughts away and clear my throat. "We need to explain everything to the council. Then, the vampires have to call off their war."

"How do we do that?" Rachel asks.

With a smug look, I toss my hair behind my back. "Let's go meet some old people."

CHAPTER 19

"That was pretty disrespectful," Drax hisses into my ear. "I hope you aren't going to—"

"Would you relax?" I say. "I'm not an idiot. It was a joke. I'm not going to disrespect the Council of Elders."

Poor Drax. Although he might be laid back most of the time, he's always stressing about other people's feelings. The guy's nice—too nice, at times. We've even gotten into arguments over how rude I can be to strangers. He has this automatic switch that throws him into a defender role—a defender of anyone but me. I guess he knows I can handle myself just fine—that, and it's hard to offend me.

Zerachu gazes around the motel room like it's infested with countless viruses. Her sister has the same look on her face. I don't blame them. Not only did the dragon tear the roof off, but leaving Mr. Mushroom alone with Riskus may not have been the brightest idea.

Riskus grins from ear to ear and shoves an entire bag of chips—the wrapper and everything—

into his mouth. Mr. Mushroom barely moves. Instead, he lies on his side next to the foot of the bed with his tongue hanging out. Around him, and stuck to his whiskers, are thousands of chip crumbs.

I fight the urge to glower at Riskus. Is he trying to kill my dog?

Beatrix shakes her foot, a stuck candy wrapper hanging on for dear life. "Is there no other place we can do this?"

Rachel touches her shoulder. "We don't have much time. This is the most private place we have right now."

Rachel's right. Outside, countless shadow dwellers—many of them former pigs—scurry around like lost elves in search of Santa's Village. People are panicking and with good reason. We're in the middle of a war, and in no time at all, the vampires will show up to start a bloodbath. Thankfully, this motel is pretty secluded in the desert. I'd rather be here than in San Halos, or any other city for that matter.

Beatrix reaches for her sister's hand, and together, they chant something incomprehensible. At once, a colorful portal lights up the room, sending my hair into a frenzy.

Zerachu takes a step toward the twirling light but stops before stepping inside. She turns sideways and looks at me from her peripheral. "Do not follow us. It vould be viser for you to stop zhe vampires."

Damn it. I was hoping to get to meet the Council of Elders at long last. Everyone talks about them like they're the coolest shit ever. Whatevs. Maybe next time.

"Fine," I say, swallowing my resentment. "I guess I'll try to get in touch with Lucius. He's our direct link to Asmodeus, and only Asmodeus can call off this war. That's asking a lot, though. I might be torn to shreds before I reach Lucius."

Zerachu and her sister exchange a look. Although they don't say anything, it's apparent by the way their faces keep stretching and their eyes keep changing sizes that they're having a telepathic conversation.

"No," Beatrix says, reaching for her sister's arm.

But Zerachu isn't having it. She pulls away and says, "Invoke zhe Shadow Peace Treaty if you must."

I wait for everyone to gasp. The look on Beatrix's face tells me this means something super important. But no one makes a peep. Why? Likely because they're as confused as I am.

"What's that?" I ask.

Zerachu's nose crinkles and she slaps her forehead. "Vhy is everyone so ignorant vhen it comes to politics?"

"I know what it is," Rachel says.

How the fuck does a brand-new witch know something that I don't? She must sense my resentment. Shrugging, she brushes her hair behind her ear and says, "What? I read a ton of my grandma's books before all of this happened."

Zerachu smiles, revealing a set of crooked teeth, and pats Rachel's head.

Beatrix shakes her head. "The council hasn't approved it—"

Zerachu swats at the air as if trying to shoo away a mosquito. "Zhere vill be no council left if zhis doesn't stop."

Beatrix purses her lips but remains silent.

Although I'm not all that sure what's going on, I do know that taking action without the council's approval is a huge no-no punishable by death or eternal imprisonment.

"So what's this peace treaty?" I ask.

Rachel clears her throat as if preparing to recite a poem. "Approved in 1245, the Shadow Peace Treaty is a political tactic used to stop a kingdom-wide war if the root cause behind the conflict is being misunderstood or misrepresented."

"Um, okay," I say. "What does that mean for us? You're saying if I invoke this treaty, everyone has to stop fighting?"

The three witches hesitate. Zerachu opens her mouth, but Rachel beats her to it. "Well, it's complicated."

"Uncomplicate it for me," I say.

"It's said that as soon as the treaty is invoked, anyone who continues to fight vanishes," Rachel says. "Like, for good, in case I didn't make that clear."

"How the hell is the whole world supposed to know it's been invoked?" I ask.

Rachel shrugs. "It's never been invoked. But apparently, everyone just... knows."

"That's reassuring," I say. "And if all one has to do is say a few words, why hasn't this been used before? There have been so many wars."

Rachel blinks at me. "I already told you. The root cause has to have been—"

"Basically," I cut her off, "what you're trying to tell me is that if a war is started by wrongfully accusing someone of something that isn't true, then the treaty can be invoked. But if two groups are fighting over territory and someone invokes the treaty, that's not fine. Right?"

Rachel nods.

"I still don't get it," I say.

Rachel's eyes go huge and she blows out a loud breath.

I nudge Drax in the ribs. "Teenagers, am I right?"

He doesn't smile. I guess this isn't the time for making jokes, considering the world might end and all. What can I say? I deal with my emotions through humor.

"Look, kid," I say before she can blow up and start accusing me of being a complete moron. "I understand how the treaty works. What I don't get is why you guys are making such a big deal out of it. Let's say I invoke it and I'm wrong, and the vampires did start all of this like everyone believes. What happens?"

Beatrix wraps an arm around Rachel's shoulder like she's trying to protect her from the horrible words that are about to come out of her mouth. "If the invoker is wrong, then they, along vith everyone they care about, will die by cuts. As many cuts as there are people who died fighting after the treaty was invoked."

Okay, that sucks big balls.

Why the fuck would anyone use this treaty?

As if reading my mind, Ace leans into me. "I guess you'd better hope you're right about Jamieson."

"I am," I say, masking my doubt. "He admitted it to me."

"Me too," Beatrix adds.

For a moment, I can't help but wonder if this is all a ploy to take me out. Wouldn't it be a perfect one? For all I know, Beatrix is still on Jamieson's side and is orchestrating this entire thing. Jamieson is manipulative and he isn't stupid. What if he convinced me that he's acting alone, when in reality, the vampires put him up to this, or vice versa? If they're working together and I invoke the treaty, we're all fucked.

As much as I want to turn on Beatrix and interrogate her, I can't. Zerachu seems to trust her, and Rachel is over the moon at having found another great-aunt.

"Well," I say, shivering at the thought of millions of paper cuts. "Let's hope it doesn't come to that."

CHAPTER 20

Beatrix and Zerachu disappear with a swooshing sound and the room goes quiet.

"I guess we're next," I say to Rachel.

She looks defeated. Either that, or afraid.

"You okay?" I ask.

She fakes a smile the way I do when I'm upset about something, but hers needs more practice.

"Oh, yeah. Of course," she says.

"Listen," I say. "If this is too much for you, you can go back home and wait it out."

She reaches into a pouch and extracts a fine green powder. "Are you kidding?" This time, her smile looks more genuine. "I want to be part of the team that saved the world."

"That's my little witch." I pat her hard on the back and a few particles of green dust fall out of her fist. "Shit, sorry."

She ignores me and with Riskus's help, starts creating a portal. I turn to Ace and Drax. They know how this is going to play out. No one is coming with me. If I show up in front of Lucius with a team at my side, it's going to come across as a threat. The guy needs to know I'm not dangerous. Well, fucking right I am. But not to him. At least not under these circumstances.

Is it risky? Of course it is. I'd much rather be meeting Asmodeus, but the dude is ancient as fuck, and there's no telling where he is. In contrast, Lucius can easily be located. How? Simple. Rachel already created a portal to locate Veerka, which means she can do it again. It's like riding a bike. Once you've done it, the subsequent attempts are a walk in the park.

What might happen when I confront Lucius about what's going on? What if he really is in on this? This is one of those things where I have to cross my fingers and hope for the best. Hopefully, I'll get through to Lucius without having to invoke the treaty.

"Same as before?" I ask, sticking my finger in the bright, spiraling portal.

Rachel nods, though she doesn't look convinced. "As soon as you go through, I have to close it."

Smart girl. I didn't even have to tell her. I'm so proud. "Good girl."

She slaps my hand away when I reach for her cheek.

All right, I get it. She cares about me a little bit and doesn't want me to get hurt.

"I'll be fine, kid."

Before I can step through, Ace grabs my wrist. "Let me come with you. If anything happens, I can get us out of there."

"Doubtful," I say. "Lucius has half the book, which means he's already been dabbling with magic. He probably has someone working for him, someone capable of casting all sorts of spells. He worked with Jamieson in the past, didn't he? We have no idea what's going on here."

Ace grinds his teeth.

I get it. I wouldn't want him going anywhere alone, either. I reach for his face, releasing a fraction of my Lure to calm him.

"I know what you're doing," he says.

"But you like it," I say.

I'm about to lean in for a kiss when Rachel says, "Gross. Get a room."

Smiling, I pull away. "If I'm not back in thirty, you can try to come find me."

This seems to be enough for him. Holding on to his belt buckle with his thumbs, he nods.

Without looking at anyone else, I turn around, shout, "Wish me luck!" and throw myself through the portal.

<h1 style="text-align:center">CHAPTER 21</h1>

My hand caresses something smooth and cold before my eyes regain their focus.

"Alexis?" Veerka hisses.

I blink several times until her naked body comes into view. She pulls at her silk sheet to cover her chest and I tug it back down.

"What the fuck are you doing here?" she says, and this time her fangs make an appearance.

I gaze around the room. It looks like something you'd find in a castle with a mahogany four-poster bed, crimson drapes, rich oak floor, and a real stone fireplace tucked away against the back wall.

I walk my fingers over the black sheet and toward her bare skin. "The better question is, what are *you* doing here?"

She slaps my hand away. "If Lucius finds you here, he will kill you."

I missed that English accent. Although a menacing scowl sits on her face, I can't help but smirk. What I wouldn't give to tear this sheet off and have my way with her.

"Do you always sleep naked?"

Fuck, Alexis. Focus. You're here for Lucius.

Without responding, she throws herself out of bed and wraps the sheet around her body. "You need to leave. Now!"

Her whisper loudens, and the aggression in her voice makes me want to throw her back into bed and get aggressive about it.

Alexis!

"All right, I'm sorry," I say. "I didn't know I'd end up here. I need to talk to Lucius."

Still scowling at me, she crosses her arms. "Right. And you thought sharing a bed with his lover would lead you into a conversation with him?"

Well, when she puts it that way, it sounds idiotic. But again, I didn't intend for this. I figured they'd be close together.

Oh, man. Can you imagine if he'd been in bed with her? If he'd been—

I grind my teeth and push the thought away. It's bad enough that I slept with a vampire; I'm not going to add to my list by including her lover.

"This whole war," I say. "It has to stop. Fae aren't responsible."

She scoffs. "Oh, please. Do you expect me to believe you? As much as I hate the corruption on our side, Alexis, I can't believe what your side has done."

"Are you fucking—" I take a deep breath to compose myself. "Veerka, come on. The fae didn't do this. If you believed that, you wouldn't have sent me looking for Devania. Jamieson's responsible for—"

"Jamieson?" she says.

His name seems to aggravate her. She tightens the sheet around her body as if trying to prevent it from falling off, which is unnecessary. "What does Jamieson have to do with any of this?"

"Let me guess. Your little lover boy didn't tell you—"

But before I can finish making fun of Lucius, the door behind me opens up, and footsteps enter the bedroom.

"What is the meaning of this?" the voice growls.

I don't even have to turn around to know it's Lucius. It's not like I know what the guy sounds like, but the hostility in his voice gives him away.

I spin around, telling myself not to welcome him with a joke about stealing his girl.

In the middle of two black wooden doors stands a tall vampire with slick blond hair, round blue eyes, and cheekbones that look like they're the result of implants. He scowls at me, his golden brows meeting somewhere in the middle of countless folds between his eyes.

Now that's an angry vampire.

That's also the face most feebles see right before they die—protruding brows, wrinkled foreheads, and an animal-like gaze that forces you to decide whether to run for it or fight and hope for the best.

The ideal outcome would be to avoid a fight altogether. After all, the reason I came here was to make friends, not enemies.

"Lucius," I say, smiling nonchalantly. "I was hoping I'd bump into you."

Before I can even mention Jamieson's name, he stretches his mouth wide open and releases a loud growl-like hiss that bounces off every wall in the room. If I were standing any closer, I'd have droplets of saliva on my shirt.

Gross.

I take it conversation is out of the question.

I clench my fists, prepared to put up one hell of a fight, when out from the darkness behind him a dozen other vampires enter, with bulging muscles and similar frowns.

"All right, boys," I say, raising my hands to either side of my face. "I came here to talk about—"

"Take her to the dungeon," Lucius growls.

"Whoa, easy," I say, but I'm out of luck. At once, every vampire in the room grabs me.

From any other perspective, you'd think we were sharing a group hug before some sporting event. They huddle close, crushing my chest.

"Little tight there, boys," I try, but no one seems to care.

As I'm dragged out of the room, I crane my neck to catch a glimpse of Veerka one last time. I'm too taken aback by what's going on to say anything intelligent, so instead, I squeeze a hand up next to my face and form the international signal for telephone and mouth, "Call me."

She rolls her eyes and runs away as the vampires lead me to my impending doom.

CHAPTER 22

I jerk from side to side, my chair wobbling about. Around my wrists and ankles is thick rope wrapped so tightly it's cutting off my circulation. I try to yell at Lucius, tell him he's got this all wrong, but that rag in my mouth doesn't help my case. He shakes his head and offers a pompous smile.

What this little prick doesn't know is that if I wanted to, I could easily snap out of my restraints and shove my foot so far up his ass I'd knock his teeth out.

But I'm not ready to reveal my true identity, at least not yet.

I peer around the room, taking in the damp stone walls, the dirt floor, the metal shackles hanging above my head, and the large wooden table with countless torture tools neatly organized in a row. Next to these tools are my wrist cuffs with both blades extracted, their tips grazing the gem of my battalion ring.

Lucius rolls up his silky sleeves and approaches the table as if trying to determine which blade might get me to talk. His fingers hover over them, but he pulls away and moves toward me.

"I'm going to offer you one chance to tell me the truth. If you cooperate, we don't have to get messy."

I scowl at him on the inside. Leaders don't often get messy—they have hired professionals who take care of torture. That Lucius is handling this on his own tells me one of two things:

1)   He's one sick motherfucker.

2)   He's got secrets he doesn't want anyone else knowing about.

Now that I think of it, both assumptions could be accurate. Vampires have ears like owls, which means there's a good chance he heard me say Jamieson's name. I hope I'm wrong, but if I'm not...

He tears the rag out of my mouth and I lick the air. The thing tastes like six-month-old water and ogre sweat. Couldn't they have washed it first? Yuck.

As I try to get the taste out of my mouth with saliva, Lucius leans in, resting his palms on my knees. "Who are you, and how did you enter my home?" he says, his voice slow and calculated.

Hundreds of thoughts race through my mind. Although my instinct is to tell him off, I bite my tongue. I'm here to make peace, not worsen the war. But how am I supposed to explain myself without giving Veerka away? He can't know she's involved.

"I was sent by Zerachu," I say.

Although this barely gives him anything to work with, her name makes his eyes bulge out.

Everyone knows Zerachu, but something about his reaction tells me there's more to this than I thought. He pulls back, stiffens his stance, and paces across the dirt floor while tugging at a ring on his middle finger.

Some people play with their jewelry while they're thinking or bored, but I get the feeling this is a nervous tick. What's he got to be nervous about? I want to question him on his discomfort, but it's better to let him do the talking.

You can get way more information out of someone when you listen.

"My sources tell me Zerachu is missing," he says plainly. "So how does a girl like you storm into my castle and claim the Great Witch sent her?"

He turns to me, a red glimmer in those bright eyes of his.

If Jamieson cut ties with Lucius, I'll look like a liar. But I'm betting Lucius already knows about Zerachu's escape. No way did Jamieson keep that information to himself, unless he had reason to.

"Didn't you hear?" I say. "She's back."

He smirks and repeats my words with such pretension. "*Back.* And how on Earth would she have escaped?"

There it is—the slip-up. That's what happens when you let people talk. They confess things without even realizing it. I never said Zerachu was imprisoned—the one vague statement I made was that she was back. Lucius is the one who referred to her disappearance as imprisonment.

"So you're aware that Jamieson imprisoned her," I say, matter-of-factly.

Rather than bulging his creepy vampire eyes out at me, a self-important smile spreads across his face. It's like that motherfucker is proud of what he's done.

"So not only do you break into my home," he says, now rubbing his palms together, "you are also privy to classified information."

"Classified?" I say. "I didn't realize you teaming up with Jamieson to take out the fae was classified."

I should be making nice, but what's the point? He's one of the bad guys. It's not like I can convince him to get his army to stand down. He wants this.

His forehead wrinkles intensely and he jabs a finger in the air. "That was never my intention!"

What the fuck is going on here? I get the feeling I'm missing something.

"Tell me who you are. Otherwise I'll pull it out of you."

He rushes to the table full of torture tools, his hair now dangling messily above his eyebrows.

Anxiety doesn't suit him. Anxiety doesn't suit any vampire. They're a lot more intimidating when they remain cool and collected. And this guy, well, he's anything but collected right now.

When I don't respond, he runs a hand through his hair, desperately trying to sweep it back. When his rounded back straightens, he raises a pair of sharp pliers and a hammer.

What a goof.

I can't wait to tear out his jugular and feed it to him.

Act a little more terrified, Alexis. He's still a vampire, and he'll put up one hell of a fight. You have to catch him off guard.

"Listen, we can talk about this," I say, trying to sound helpless.

"I already gave you that opportunity," he says, stepping toward me.

I squeeze the chair's armrests, prepared to shatter the thing into pieces, when a heavy door creaks open in the distance. Lucius stops and turns around.

"I specifically ordered that I not be disturbed!" he shouts.

Who the hell would have the balls to enter after being given orders from Lucius?

Someone with a death wish, that's who.

But as the figure comes into view, I'm taken aback. Out from the darkness comes Veerka clad in a silk red dress and shoes to match. Her blond hair sits neatly at the back of her head, held together by black pins adorned with sparkling crimson gems.

My knightess in shining armor.

"Darling, what are you doing here?" Lucius

hisses.

Although upset by her disobedience, he appears elated by her presence.

"Allow me to join you, my love," she says. "I want to see this bitch suffer for entering our home."

Lucius smiles while my stomach sinks.

What the fuck, Veerka?

She marches straight for me, tightens a fist, and clocks me in the face.

Sparkles float in front of my eyes for a few seconds until I blink them away.

Well, that was unexpected.

I lower my head and glower at her.

"I know this woman," Veerka says. "She's working alongside Devania."

What in the actual fuck? She's the one who told me to find Devania! And now she's going to use that against me?

Lucius elevates his chin and smiles down at me. "Is that so?"

Veerka, you fucking bitch!

How could she do this to me? The better question is, why didn't I see this coming? She's a vampire. A filthy, worthless vampire. I shouldn't have expected her to be any different from the others.

As much as I want to ream her out for betraying me, I can't bring myself to do it. Besides, even if I tried, no way would Lucius take my word over hers. She has him wrapped around her little finger.

"Has she told you anything?" Veerka asks.

Lucius, looking hypnotized by his lust for his lover, stares at her in silence.

"Are you all right, my dear?" she asks.

Still smiling, he moves at the speed of light and appears in front of her. He flattens a palm against her lower back and draws her in closer, his lips hovering in front of hers. He reaches for her hand—the same one she used to punch me in the face with—and licks off the blood.

"You, my darling, are so incredibly sexy," he says.

She smiles back, then kisses him hard and nibbles his lower lip.

The two of them go on snapping their jaws at each other like wild animals.

"Oh, for fuck's sake," I say. "Can you two get on with it so I don't have to watch this nauseating vampire love?"

Veerka turns to me and lowers her head until she looks like a vampire I don't recognize. Her forehead wrinkles and her teeth lengthen until they extend beyond her bottom lip.

"Do you hear that, darling?" she says. "Our toy would like to be played with now."

I can't believe this is happening. What am I supposed to do? Get up and attack them both? As much as I hate Veerka right now, I can't bring myself to hurt her.

Yes, you can, Alexis. You were on the verge of

wiping her out when Jamieson gave you the order. Nothing has changed.

The truth is, everything has changed. Veerka convinced me that she was one of us—one of the good guys. If that's even what I am. Why would she have sent me on a wild goose chase after Devania?

That's when it hits me.

She wanted me distracted. This must have been her plan all along—to keep me out of Lucius's way while he and Jamieson went about completing their evil plan.

Without grabbing a tool, she appears in front of me and lowers her face to mine. Her fangs, having once been dangerously sexy next to my neck, now generate animosity in me.

Without warning, she slashes her nails across my thigh, cutting right through my jeans and several layers of skin. I wince as blood spills out of my pants, soaking them instantly.

"What the hell do you want," I say, but she backhands me across the face, and my right ear rings.

If this were some sort of kinky foreplay, it would be pretty hot, but it's nothing like that. This bitch is fucking everything up.

I part my lips to say something, but she punches me square in the face this time, breaking my nose. I blink hard as tears spill out of my eyes.

Lucius comes at me, his fist smashing me in the jaw. Something unhinges, so I open my mouth to

190

snap it back in place.

He hits me again and my right eye swells up so badly that I can't see out of it.

"Who are you, really?" he says.

My good eye rolls toward Veerka, but I don't tell him.

"Why are you doing this?" I say. "I was sent here to stop the war. Can we please be adults and talk about this?"

"Shut her up," Lucius says, wiggling a finger at his lover.

Veerka reaches for the filthy rag lying in the dirt and shoves it back into my mouth. Before pulling away, she digs her nails into my throat, scraping away pieces of skin.

All right, I've had it. I guess it's time to use muscle. I'm about to stand up and break the chair in half when Veerka lets out a playful giggle and strolls across the torture chamber like the insane lunatic that she is.

"Oh, Lucius," she says, pulling his body against hers. "I haven't felt this alive since, well, I can't remember."

"Do you enjoy this, my love?" he asks.

Rather than say anything, she kisses him furiously, her breath blowing hard out through her nostrils.

"You are so powerful, so intelligent to have come up with all of this." She runs her hands along his bicep, then playfully digs her fangs into his shoulder.

His eyes flutter and he licks his lips.

Fucking gross.

As she sucks on his neck and chest, he smiles up at the concrete ceiling. "I didn't foresee the End of the Divide, but it will do."

She moans, a sucking his neck as she moves to his ear. She licks it, which is repulsive, and tugs at his hair. "I want you so badly when you talk like this," she says. "Tell me more."

Still staring at the ceiling in a daze, Lucius laughs. "It was easy, really. Jamieson will do anything to gain power. He has been a pawn in all of this. I promised him an army to go after what he's been wanting for a long time—the Heart of Danu and the *Book of Origin* in exchange for his help. His help in starting a war. With my soldiers, he managed to obtain half of the book from—" He laughs when Veerka squeezes her grip around his throat. "From a little witch and her friends."

"Oh, baby," Veerka says, gripping his ass this time. "You excite me."

He smiles down at his cherished possession and continues. "He obtained the other half only and the Heart of Danu recently with the help of that witch."

She runs a sharp claw across his temple. "Why a war, my love?"

"Simple, really. With the vampires and the fae blaming each other, the world is absolute chaos. After much bloodshed, all I have to do is share with the world that Asmodeus declared an unnecessary war, and everyone will turn on him."

"How is it unnecessary?" she asks.

Lucius scoffs like it's obvious. "Jamieson will take the fall for this, and Asmodeus will look like a fool."

Sitting quietly, I can't help but wonder—why did the council blame vampires in the first place? But then it hits me. Vampires were the army Jamieson was using. He used them to obtain the first half of the *Book of Origin*, and then used them to help him orchestrate the whole Beatrix and Zerachu swap.

From where the council sits, vampires have been meddling in all of this since before the war started.

Who else could they possibly blame? And with how delicate the peace treaty is between vampires and the rest of us shadow dwellers, it was the perfect plan.

But why was Asmodeus the first to declare war? That was a bad move on his part, but from his perspective, maybe he thought Zerachu had turned on her own people, and the council was simply looking for a scapegoat. He did what any leader would have done to prevent the slaughter of his people.

Was it a bit rash? Kind of. But everyone knows that Asmodeus isn't to be trifled with. When the Dark Prince feels as though his people are being wrongfully targeted, he's going to fight back.

Basically, dumb-fuck Lucius here and asshole Jamieson are responsible for the deaths of countless people. And for what? For power.

"He will most certainly look like a fool," Veerka says. She pulls away, almost hopping in one spot. "Oh, my brilliant man! You are going to take his place, aren't you? Oh, imagine the power."

She yanks on the collar of his shirt and shoves her tongue inside his mouth.

I turn away and hold back my vomit.

When they're finished making out, Lucius runs his thumb across Veerka's delicate face and the corner of his lips pulls up. "Once Asmodeus has been dethroned, I will take my rightful place as leader of the world, and you, my queen, will rule by my side."

When she doesn't respond, his smile dissipates and transforms into a look of disgust.

Shit, what did I miss? What's going on? I crane my neck, attempting to catch a glimpse of Veerka's face, and instead, find myself standing next to a short blue-skinned creature with long, bunny-like ears above its head. Its whiskers twitch as it focuses on what appears to be a blue leather notebook. Its claws, small and catlike, wrap around the notebook, holding it firmly in place.

Holy shit. Is that a Truskin? I've never seen one in person—only in fae court. They're considered *truth demons*. Everything they jot down in their little journals is considered a fact and evidence that can be used in a court of law. You could even go as far as to say that their notes are more reliable than video footage and photography. Why? Unlike media, their notes can't be altered. Once written down, they harden into gold cursive. You can't even tear their notebook's pages out.

Truskins also never lie, which is why they're so valuable to the fae justice system. They're unbiased and only note facts. Although I've never seen it for myself, rumor has it that if a Truskin were to even attempt to fib, they would burst into flames.

I stare at the strange-looking creature with its whiskers twitching every few seconds and its small, silver eyes darting between its notebook and Lucius.

Lucius's vampiric scowl returns, and he takes a step toward the Truskin. "Is that—"

Veerka raises her chin, observing Lucius from behind the tip of her nose.

Okay, I didn't see this coming.

"You bitch!" he shouts, his voice resonating throughout the torture chamber.

"Deliver the message to the council!" Veerka says, and the Truskin disappears in a flash.

Before she can rush out of the chamber, Lucius grabs her by the hair, exposing her neck. His fangs, sharp yellow daggers shimmering next to a lit sconce, hover menacingly over her carotid artery. If there's one way to make a vampire suffer, it's to let them bleed out entirely before severing their head. Lucius knows this. He's the master of torture and always seeks out new ways of killing traitors.

Veerka struggles, but he's too strong.

"Let her go!" I shout.

With a bowed head, he averts his shadowed gaze toward me. "You're in on this, aren't you?"

"She had nothing to do with this!" Veerka hisses, her fangs lengthening into her plush bottom lip.

"Why would you want to protect—" he says, but cuts himself short.

Shit.

The wrinkles on his forehead deepen and his brows meet above the bridge of his nose. "This whole time," he mutters, more to himself than anyone else. He glowers at me, baring his fangs. "You care for her, don't you?"

When I don't respond, he opens his mouth wide and releases a deafening vampiric growl.

That's my cue.

Yelling back, I stand up, the chair under me snapping into a dozen pieces. It's enough to pull his attention away from Veerka's throat, which he's about to shred with his razor-sharp teeth.

The chair's armrest dangles at my side, one end still fastened to my wrist with rope. The other end—the one scraping the dirt floor—isn't exactly sharp, but it's pointed, which is all I need.

As much as I want to throw it at him, I'm not an idiot. Vampires are too fast for me, and with my luck, he'll swing Veerka in front of him and I'll be responsible for her death. Well, final death.

Veerka must sense my thoughts. In clear desperation, she watches my every move, likely wondering if I'm considering killing them both. Lucius laughs and pulls Veerka in front of his chest, holding her from behind.

Fuck.

"Take your best shot," he says.

At this point, maybe that's exactly what I have to do.

Chapter 23

It's one of those things you'd call a calculated risk.

I have a good feeling this is going to work, but I can't be sure. The thing with calculated risks is that even though the outcome may not turn out as you'd hoped, you have to consider every possibility beforehand.

There are several outcomes in this scenario:

1)   I kill Veerka, along with Lucius.
2)   I save Veerka.
3)   I kill only Veerka and Lucius attacks me.
4)   I miss them both and they get away.

Another option would be to let them both go, but I can't do that to Veerka. I can't let Lucius keep her as one of his torture toys. I know her, and she'd rather die.

Without putting too much thought into it, I swing my arm as hard as I can, throwing the pointed armrest in a curved fashion. It twirls through the air like a throwing knife and bounces off the stone wall behind Lucius.

When he realizes it skimmed his shoulder, he

smirks, his cheeks ballooning as if holding back a scoff. "If that was your best shot—"

But he stops talking and lowers his head over Veerka's shoulder. She stands quietly, her fingers wrapped around the massive piece of wood protruding from her belly.

It takes him a second to notice that he and Veerka are pinned together. He parts his lips, black blood spilling out, and searches the room as if trying to figure out how to get out of this one.

But there's no getting out of it. I got him right in the heart.

Without warning, he bursts into a thick cloud of ash, coating Veerka's blond hair with a powdery gray dust. She coughs and swats at the air, and I move toward her.

"Sorry about that," I say, yanking the black-stained wood out from her back.

She cries out in pain and falls to her knees, her face resting in her palms.

I want to feel sorry for her, but after the stunt she pulled, I can't help but feel resentment. How was it so easy for her to act as though she hated me? Am I being childish? Yeah, probably. She's centuries old. It makes sense that she'd have mastered the art of deception. I can't punish her for that. If anything, I should be happy. She did it to save me.

"Sorry about the pain," I say. "But it was either kill him from behind or kill you both from the front.

Bouncing it off the wall was the only way to get you both at the right angle."

She presses hard on the open hole in her stomach. "Quite the aim you have."

"It was dumb luck," I say. "Do you need anything for your wound?"

She shakes her head.

To my surprise, the hole that sat in the middle of her stomach seconds ago is now congealed. I'm not surprised—I've been around long enough to know that vampires have a great recovery system. I guess in some ways, we're similar except that I heal way faster and my feeding process is a whole lot more fun.

That, and I'm not dead on the inside. At least not physically.

"I'm sorry, too," she says at last, pointing at her face.

She's referring to the bruising on my face.

"It's okay," I say. "It was kind of hot."

Rolling her eyes, she stands up and brushes pieces of dirt off her silky dress. "You're sick, you know that?"

I do know that, and I'm not ashamed of it.

"So what was up with that little Truskin goblin?" I say. "Pretty fucking brilliant. Where'd you find him? I heard only the council is allowed to use them for investigations."

"First of all," she says, "Truskins aren't goblins."

I'm surprised to hear a vampire correct the

name of a fae species.

"Second, that wasn't my doing. I thought you brought him here."

How the hell does any of this make sense? If Veerka didn't plan for this, who did? It's not like anyone knew where to find us. Lucius made sure of that. He brought us deep into his basement—into some secluded room.

It doesn't matter. What matters is that we get the hell out of dodge and fast.

"How do we get out of here?" I ask.

She hesitates. "We can't."

"What's that supposed to mean?"

"Lucius's men were given specific orders to keep you contained at all costs."

They may have their orders, but I have my Lure. Then again, there's likely way too many of them, and although the stunt I pulled against Jamieson was pretty badass, I don't know how to replicate it. For all I know, it was a onetime escape plan sent by my father.

"Well, I can't sit here all night—" I start, but without warning, Ace appears next to me.

Veerka extracts her fangs and hisses at him like a snake caught off guard. Ace, probably thinking Veerka's the enemy, clenches his fists as two curved horns emerge from his head. His wings, black and mighty, expand wide enough to fill the room.

I throw my arms out on either side of me to stop

the two from killing each other. "Relax."

Neither of them appears convinced, so I add, "We're all on the same side."

Veerka is the first to wipe the menacing scowl off her face, while Ace takes a little longer. Slowly, he folds his wings back, but only enough to appease me. It's apparent that he wants nothing to do with a vampire, and with the war that's going on, that makes sense.

His eyes dart from side to side as if he's attempting to connect puzzle pieces.

"Veerka and I go way back," I say.

He rubs his dark stubbled chin—pensive is a hot look on him—and points at Veerka. "I recognize you."

Veerka scoffs like a celebrity being told they look familiar. "Everyone knows me."

"No, not as a leader. As someone from a long time ago." He pauses, then rotates his body from left to right until stopping to face me. "Didn't you two—"

"Yeah," I say.

This seems to upset Veerka. She steps forward, visible folds wrinkling her forehead, and says, "How long have you two known each other?"

It's like I'm being accused of cheating on her, or on him. Or something.

"It's complicated," I cut in before Ace can go on about how he's known me his entire life. "I met Ace a few days ago. He knew me as a child."

"And as a teenager, as an adult—" he starts.

"It doesn't matter," I cut him off.

Why am I so adamant about protecting Veerka's feelings?

The two of them stare at each other like feral cats on the verge of starting a YouTube-worthy brawl.

And I thought I was the jealous type. These two look like they want to destroy each other. Maybe a good threesome is all they need. I smile absentmindedly, my mind wandering as I imagine all sorts of naughty things.

Alexis, would you focus?

It's hard to focus when standing right in front of me are two people I'm extremely attracted to.

Ace turns to me and reaches for the bruising on my face. "Do you need—"

"I'm good," I say before he can ask if I need to feed.

As much as I'd love to fuck Ace again, I don't want to add fuel to the fire. Besides, these cuts and bruises should be gone any time now. I don't need to feed every time I'm injured, though I wouldn't say no to the offer were this any other situation.

"So what's the game plan?" I say. "Any word from Zerachu and Beatrix?"

"Actually, yeah," he says. "That's why I'm here early."

"Early," I blurt. "By what? Two minutes?"

He gives me a blank stare and says, "I hope you

204

intend to set aside that attitude of yours."

What the fuck is that supposed to mean? I'm about to give him a piece of my mind when he adds, "Because you're about to meet the council."

I glance sideways at Veerka, who flicks her wrist and says, "Go on. I'll keep things calm on my side. It's only a matter of time before the vampires begin to question Lucius's whereabouts."

"Then there's no time to waste," Ace says. He reaches for my arm, and everything around us vanishes.

Chapter 24

"I thought we were meeting the council," I say.

Ace bows his head like he's ashamed of something. Either that, or he's got bad news. "We will. But first, I need to show you something."

Beatrix and Zerachu give him a nod of approval. Are they in on this?

"I don't see what could be more important than talking to—" But before I can finish, Ace touches my shoulder and everything around us disappears.

In a flash, I'm standing on PolyKure Inc., the same building we stood on minutes before the Interruptus spell. But this time, the sun doesn't cast a beautiful orange glow across cotton candy clouds. Instead, a dull gray sky floats above us, darkening as the sun begins to set. But it isn't the sky that has my attention, it's the scene below us.

San Halos is known for being a busy place, especially at night. We're known for it. But what I see below is far from lively. Smoke blows in all directions as it exits car hoods, shattered windows, and metallic garbage bins. Where you'd see taxis swerving in and out of traffic, there are streets full of parked cars, most of which are either damaged or on fire.

The whole thing looks like something out of a postapocalyptic movie.

Every few seconds, a shadow dweller runs out, either fleeing from something or chasing after someone else. Packs of vampires move about swiftly, catching anyone they can and feeding off of them like packs of wolves ganging up on a helpless animal.

Shrieks bounce off the city's buildings, followed by laughter and the sound of flesh tearing.

"Why are you showing me this?" I ask.

Ace raises his arm and examines his watch. "Because in exactly one hour, the Interruptus spell is going to wear off."

"So, humans are going to come home to this?"

He nods, looking defeated. "This is worldwide."

"I still don't get why you're showing this to me. It's not like I have the power to do anything. Can't Beatrix and Zerachu cast some other spell to get us out of this whole mess?"

He shakes his head. "It isn't that simple. It took the entire Council of Elders to cast the Interruptus spell in the first place."

Pinching the bridge of my nose, I breathe out. If there's one thing I hate (okay, I hate a lot of things) it's having to repeat the same question nonstop. "I don't want to be a bitch, Ace, so I'm going to ask you nicely one last time. After that, all bets are off. Why are you showing this to *me*?"

"Something about a Truskin," he says. "The council wants to hear your statement before making any official decision."

"What decision?" I ask.

He shrugs. "I'm only the messenger. Zerachu can give you more details."

And with that, we're back in the remains of our motel room.

"Zhere you are," Zerachu says, waving a hand to get me to hurry.

Behind her is a wide spinning portal that looks like it's about to close.

Apparently, I'm going in there. And judging by the big-eyed look on her face, I don't have time to question it. I glance back at my friends to give them the *Wish me luck* look before following Zerachu into the portal.

Within a split second, I'm standing inside a hall that looks like an abandoned subway station.

Gazing around, I cock a brow. "*This* is supposed to be where the almighty council resides?"

Zerachu smacks me hard on the shoulder, which I'm certain means *Shut your trap*. I can see why Rachel's already so bonded with her; she gives off that mean-but-caring grandmother vibe. For a brief moment, I imagine both Zerachu and Beatrix turning on me and handing me over to Jamieson for some deal they can't refuse.

It wouldn't be so farfetched.

Shut your brain trap, Alexis.

It isn't my fault. Being a thousand years old makes you envision every possible scenario. That's what happens when you've seen almost *every possible scenario*. Family members betraying one another, kids turning out to be sociopaths, seemingly innocent people turning violent.

I've seen it all, and with how sketchy this place looks, my idea might not be so far off.

"Seriously, what is this place?" I ask.

Zerachu gives me the stink-eye like I'm not supposed to question the Elders and their ways. But this doesn't look like anything the Elders would want sitting outside their council room. It's shabby and downright—

A brown rat scurries over my toes and around Beatrix's ankles.

"Oh, cute—" I start, but Beatrix's ear-destroying shriek fills up the surrounding space.

"Sister!" Zerachu hisses.

Beatrix glowers at the rat as its chubby butt and hairless tail disappear into a hole in the wall.

"That was a bit dramatic," I say.

Her scowl turns on me like I'm the villain in all of this.

"Enough," Zerachu says. "Let's focus on getting to zhe council."

"And where would that be?" I say, but no one responds.

Up ahead are rusted tracks surrounded by white porcelain tiled walls. Most of the tiles have either fallen off or cracked. Across the floor there appears to be either mold or algae, and the smell makes me feel like I'm standing next to a one-hundred-year-old humidifier.

I part my lips to comment on how this place looks worse than my apartment when a dozen bats fly overhead, releasing faint clicking noises—something I learned is a distinct chirp too high pitched for most people to hear.

To my surprise, Beatrix doesn't react to these creatures. She ignores them and instead walks up to the abandoned tracks. She clears her throat, sticks a finger in the air, and says, "*Introitus.*"

At once, a humming sound fills the station, followed by the high-pitched squealing of brakes. The subway tunnel, which was pitch black seconds ago, fills up with a bright yellow glow that expands as the sound gets louder.

Out from the darkness comes a subway train—something you'd think was designed by Dracula. It's jet black and looks medieval with its sharp-edged architecture, its triangular windows, and its hundreds of cobwebs.

The train stops right in front of Beatrix and opens its doors.

She swings around, her dress following her movement, and says, "Well? What the hell are you two waiting for?"

Zerachu jerks her head sideways as if to say, *Follow me*, and follows her sister into the subway car. I step inside, ducking before walking face-first into a huge spider web, and end up standing in an empty car.

"Where's the rest of the party" I ask.

The twins don't seem too impressed by my sense of humor.

They give each other a silent look, no doubt telepathically saying something along the lines of, *What a tool.*

"Hold on tight," Beatrix says.

I scoff. "With how slow that train pulled up? I don't see why—"

The train takes off so fast I'm thrown to the back of the railcar. As I soar through the air, my legs catch one of the train's support poles, making me twirl midair like a fucking rag doll. When I'm done spinning, I smash headfirst into the backdoor, leaving behind a huge dent the shape of my face.

Well, that was embarrassing.

I blink away the countless stars in front of my eyes, grab onto one of the seat's rusted armrests, and pull myself up. With my grip now tightly fastened around a support pole, I say, "You could have been more specific about the need to hold on tight."

Beatrix smiles, but doesn't respond. She turns away and faces the front of the train as we zoom through the dark tunnels, the train shaking and rattling on the tracks. The only thing missing is an open window to send her hair floating behind her back.

"Approaching, hold on," she says.

This time, I do as I'm told and squeeze the support pole so tightly it bends. The change in speed makes me take a few steps forward, but at least this time I didn't smash my head into anything.

"Why are we taking some creepy-ass train to meet the Elders?" I ask. "Seems weird to me."

All right, my paranoia is back.

Where are they *really* taking me? To meet Hades?

"It might appear odd," Zerachu says before her sister can chime in, "but zis is how zhe council remains safe. Vith zhe Train of Intention."

"Train of Intention," I mutter.

"If your intentions are bad," she continues, "you cannot enter zhe Court."

And by Court, she doesn't mean a court of law. I've heard people refer to the Court of Elders many times before. I suppose it's where they gather, or where they stay. Hell if I know.

"So what would have happened if my intentions were bad?" I ask.

The twin witches exchange a strange look that has me wishing I hadn't asked the question. Beatrix aims her stare at the back window of the railcar, right above my head dent.

I crane my neck to see what she's focusing on, but all I see is another railcar behind us.

"What?" I ask.

"Look closely," she says.

Sighing, I move closer to the window, rub the bit of condensation away, and peer through. Inside the other railcar is nothing but filth. Absolute filth. I can't even make out the seats because they're caked in... holy shit. Is that ash? And skeletons?

I swing around to find both witches smirking at me.

"One hell of a way to go," Beatrix says.

"You brought me on here without telling me?" I snap.

"Of course we did," Beatrix says. "Your reputation precedes you, succubus. You're self-centered, cold—"

I raise my palm. "Okay, I get it. You were afraid I might second-guess my intentions."

I can't even be angry with them. They're right. There's a good chance I wouldn't have stepped foot on this train had I known I could be scorched.

"One hell of a security system," I mumble.

The doors open with a loud swoosh and we step out into another subway station. Unlike the other one, this one is much cleaner. Much shinier. The wall tiles are so clean that they sparkle, as does the floor.

"Come on," Beatrix says. Her heels click as she guides us across the main platform and up to enormous wooden double doors.

Zerachu walks past her, slouches her posture, and knocks on the door with a rhythm.

At once, a projection of a woman's face appears overhead. She looks down at us, her long, braided, golden hair resting over one shoulder. In it are silver clasps made of what appear to be expensive metals, and around her neck is a matching pendant.

It looks like she's about to recite some scripted line, but when she spots Zerachu, her almond-shaped eyes widen slightly. "Zerachu," she says.

"Yes, ve're back," Zerachu responds.

Half of the woman's face disappears when she turns to speak to someone, and as soon as she returns, she smiles awkwardly, bows her head, and says, "Please, enter."

And with that, the two doors creak open, drawing in a blinding light.

Chapter 25

Squinting hard, I half expect to step out onto a path made of clouds. Instead, we're welcomed by a bright, cloudless turquoise sky and interlocking pavers that guide us up a slope. On either side of the large slope are huge concrete walls covered in moss and insects. It's unusually charming.

Without wasting any time, Zerachu pulls her dress up—something she must have magically conjured when I was away—and walks up the path like she's late catching her bus. Beatrix and I follow her up, and the moment I reach the top, my jaw goes slack.

Okay, sure, it isn't Mount Olympus, but holy fuck.

The path continues for at least a mile, reminding me of the yellow brick road in *The Wizard of Oz*. At the far end, positioned between two perfectly manicured hills, is a castle surrounded by hedges of all shapes and sizes, people atop galloping horses, and a crystal clear moat.

"And I've never been invited here because...?" I say.

Zerachu grunts. "You aren't royalty."

I blow air out of my mouth. "I see how it is."

The witches ignore me and lead me up to the castle, across its wooden bridge, and through its colossal doors. To my surprise, a familiar face is there to greet us.

"Devania," I say.

She smiles sweetly at me, her golden eyes matching the sunlight's rays. Her long hair, as bright red as I remember, accentuates her rosy cheeks. It's hard to grasp that someone as sweet-looking as her runs the underground rebellion.

She looks like a princess who wouldn't harm a fly. When no one says anything, she extends a soft pale hand and I grab it gently.

"Pleased to finally meet you in person," she says.

Pleasure's all mine.

When I catch myself taking in her curves, I clear my throat and look away. "Um, same here."

She spins around, her green cloak swiftly sweeping across the floor and says, "Come."

Our footsteps echo as we follow her through the castle halls and into a room filled with fancy-looking shadow dwellers, some of which are fae types that I've never seen before. They sit behind a moon-shaped table constructed of marble, their eyes shifting toward me the moment I step inside.

"Is this the succubus?" comes a deep, rumbly

voice.

I turn to spot an elf with long pointed ears, a square jaw, and a decorative feather sticking out of his long braided green hair. He's clad in silver attire that matches his smooth, glistening face.

Devania offers a brief nod before taking her seat across the room.

Well, this is awkward. Don't get me wrong, I love attention as much as the next girl, but they're all staring at me with judgy eyes.

One old-looking witch with a wrinkled chin and mismatched eyebrows leans into the gentleman next to her and whispers something inaudible.

What the hell is going on here?

Finally, she clears her throat. "Alexis Rayne, do you hereby attest to witnessing Lucius Retnich violate the shadow dwellers' peace treaty?"

By peace treaty, I assume she means treaty that was set in place by the Council of Elders centuries ago. It states that all shadow dwellers must live in harmony, well, at a high level. The council doesn't give a shit about petty arguments or fights between species. The whole point of the treaty was to ensure that no one would ever again start another war between the clans, especially the vampires.

Asmodeus has always refused to join the council, hence why the power struggle between vampires and all other shadow dwellers still remains.

"Y-yes," I say. "He was working with Jamieson."

The old witch shuffles through her papers, repositions her crooked thin-framed glasses on the bridge of her nose, and in a high-pitched and croaky voice, says, "As per the testimony of Zycar"—she waves a wrinkled hand in the direction of the same Truskin I met in Lucius's torture chamber—"Jamieson has been reprimanded and banished to Hellfire City to serve a lifelong sentence."

I slap a hand over my mouth to hold back an excited chuckle.

Son of a bitch finally got what he deserved.

Focus, Alexis.

Straightening my posture, I clear my throat. "And what of Asmodeus? Was he aware of any of this?"

The old woman shakes her head, but before she can speak, a short man with medallion-yellow skin, deep-set purple eyes, and a cone-shaped head stands up, his height barely increasing. He stares straight ahead as if observing a projection only visible to him.

"Asmodeus is being debriefed on the situation as we speak," he says. He parts his thin yellow lips but then seals them shut and nods.

What the hell is this guy? Some type of reporter fae? It's like he's being given messages through invisible waves in real time. "Yes, yes, understood," he says.

No one in the council room seems taken aback

by his behavior, which leads me to believe he does this all the time. It makes sense, after all, that everyone in here would possess some super cool power they can contribute.

I wonder what the tiny old woman can do.

My eyes shift back to the short yellow fae when he screeches his chair back into place and sits down. "Asmodeus was not aware of Lucius's part in the matter. He was falsely led to believe that the fae were responsible for the war."

"He should have further investigated," someone says.

"Enough," the yellow man responds. "There is no use placing blame on anyone, especially not Asmodeus. We have remained at peace for centuries."

"And he should have better control of his people," says a pineapple-shaped creature.

From where I'm standing, he looks like a rock. A bit like Drax's friend, but rounder and with leaves sprouting from his head. When he leans back into his chair, little stone chips flake off his back.

"Lucius represents Asmodeus. Someone must be held accountable for all the lives—"

The Elders continue to bicker back and forth until eventually, I clear my throat and everyone turns my way. "Um, can I say something?"

No one responds, which I suppose is a response in itself.

"Isn't the council supposed to be all about peace

and making the world better?" I say. Half of the council looks intrigued, while the other half glares scornfully my way.

I know what *that* half is thinking: why are we letting some no-name succubus tell the Council of Elders how to do their jobs?

It's apparent that they're irritated, so I cut to the chase. "Going after Asmodeus is going to cause an even bigger war than the one we just had. We already have to find a solution to fix the chaos that unfolded. Wouldn't it be better to focus on a solution? Assign a new vampire leader to take Lucius's place?"

The pineapple fae scoffs. "And do you have a proposition for us, succubus? Asmodeus assigns his leaders—"

"Actually," says the short yellow reporter man. He stares off again as if stuck in a dream and presses a finger over his right droopy ear. "As a way of making amends, Asmodeus has proposed we assign that role."

My eyes involuntarily dart toward Devania at the far back of the room. But rather than share my excitement, she hardens her features. It doesn't take a genius to know she doesn't want anyone knowing she has ties to Veerka.

Not only could that harm her reputation as the leader of the underground rebellion, but it could also gravely harm Veerka if anyone found out she was working with someone like Devania. They're a proud bunch, those vampires, and while they might have agreed to a peace treaty centuries ago, most of them still think themselves above fae and witches.

"Um, so what if I have a suggestion?" I ask.

A few forced chuckles resonate off the castle's stone walls.

"Would you stop with your condescending laughs and stares?" I say.

I may as well have sucked all the air out of the room.

"I know a vampire who would be a great fit for the position. And before you start interrogating me on how I know her, let me say this—on second thought, it isn't any of your business."

Zerachu nudges me in the ribs, but I swat her away like an annoying fly.

A few of them exchange looks, but no one speaks.

Did I cross a line? Are they going to banish me into oblivion?

Finally, the old witch removes her glasses and places them next to what appears to be a glass of freshly boiled potion. "Being that you are responsible for extracting a confession out of Lucius, we will allow your suggestion."

Responsible? How am I responsible? The dude strapped me down, prepared to torture me. Veerka's the one who got the confession, and then Zycar, the Truskin demon, is the one who saved all of our asses.

But hey, if they think I saved the world, maybe I should shut my mouth and go with it. They are, after all, letting me propose a new vampire leader. If I open my big mouth now, they might revoke their offering.

I glance briefly toward the Truskin, but he isn't the one who captures my attention. Next to him, Devania sits back in her chair, picking at invisible lint on her dress. She watches me, crosses her legs, then winks.

Holy shit.

She did this. She sent the Truskin to follow me. How did she do that? I reach for my Battalion ring, rubbing its crimson gem, and a playful smirk pulls at the corner of her mouth.

Well, shit.

"Miss Rayne?" asks the pineapple fae.

The woman with long golden hair from the projection earlier leans forward, her breasts resting on the tabletop. When I find myself staring, I blink hard and look away.

Fuck. I'm already hungry again, and with how powerful the council is, I shouldn't be having thoughts like this right now. Some of them may be mind readers.

"I'd like to nominate Veerka Vanmorte," I say.

Several noses crinkle as if I just spat in everyone's drinks.

"Lucius's lover?" someone asks.

I clench my fists but remind myself that no one can know about Veerka. As much as I want to trust the council, it wouldn't be safe to tell them about Veerka's involvement. Traitors are everywhere, and if word gets out that Veerka played a part in Lucius's death, every vampire in the world will want her head.

"She was as corrupt as he was," someone says, "if not worse."

"I stand by my opinion," I say.

The members of the council lean forward and begin bickering among themselves. Finally, the members sit tall, reposition themselves, and take aim at Zerachu.

"Zerachu," says the golden-haired woman. "You know this succubus better than we do. What say you of her suggestion?"

Zerachu shifts the weight of her body onto her right leg and sizes me up. "She's selfish, ignorant, and a real pain in my ass."

"Not helping," I mutter.

"She may be rough around zhe edges," Zerachu says, "but zhis woman saved my life."

Oh, yeah, I did do that. I guess I am kind of responsible for saving the world.

"In fact, she saved many lives and nearly died trying." She reaches for her sister's hand. "If she says zhis Veerka person is zhe best fit for zhe position, zhen I trust her decision vith my life."

The golden-haired woman pulls her long braid

over one shoulder, grabs what appears to be a gavel made of bone, and knocks it three times against the council's table.

"Let it be known that Veerka Vanmorte is to be appointed leader of the vampires for the geographical region of America."

Tempted to pump a fist in the air, I bite my tongue and nod briefly as a way of expressing my gratitude. Half of the council members stand up, fix the folds in their clothing, and elevate their chins.

"Wait," I say. "What about the world? It's chaos out there. Has anyone officially declared the war over? Aren't humans scheduled to come back any minute?"

The stunning woman with the long golden braid smiles at me, and it takes all my willpower not to think dirty thoughts. "Zerachu has already proposed a solution to this and the council has approved the decision."

I turn to Zerachu. She shrugs nonchalantly and says, "Vat?"

"What's your big master plan for cleaning up a fu—" I force a smile at the Elders. "A freaking postapocalyptic world? It's chaos out there. What could you possibly do to fix that?"

"Meeting adjourned," someone says loudly, and the room begins to clear.

A twinkle flashes in Beatrix's eyes.

"Okay, what's going on here?" I say.

"Are you ready for something cool?" Zerachu

asks.

The word *cool* comes out sounding funny, as if it's the first time she's ever used it.

"Something cool?" I ask. "People were slaughtered, Zerachu. I don't see what solution you have up your sleeve that you could describe as *cool*."

She grins malevolently and locks arms with her sister, the two of them looking like evil twins.

"All right," I say. "Show me."

CHAPTER 26

"Wait, are you serious right now?" Rachel dances on the spot like a seven-year-old about to receive a brand new video game.

"Yeah, good question," I say, stepping in front of her. "You can't be serious."

Zerachu and Beatrix remain tight-lipped. Okay, so they *are* being serious about this. The idea itself isn't horrible—I'm being overprotective. What if something goes wrong? This is a super powerful spell. What if it backfires and Rachel is somehow harmed?

"Vould you relax?" Zerachu says like she's known me my entire life.

Is it that obvious when I'm freaking out inside?

"It may be dangerous," she admits, "but you have to look at zhe big picture here, Alexis. If ve don't do zhis... you are all going to suffer."

I clench a fist. "Is that a threat?"

Both Ace and Drax reach for my shoulders.

"Alex, it isn't a threat," Drax says. "Haven't you

seen the world? Shit's bad. If we don't do this, we're all doomed. All of us. The electrical grid is about to get fried, countless people are dead. You really wanna live in a world like that?"

I hate it when Drax's right. It's not like we have a choice. I'm on the verge of asking them about all the possible dangers of this spell, but I decide against it. If we have no choice, what's the point adding to my anxiety?

"Will we remember?" I ask.

Beatrix extracts a small vile of green liquid from the leather belt around her waist. "Anyone standing within ten feet of the spellcasters will remember. Oh, and anyone standing within the Elder Court. That castle has so many enchantment spells it's a wonder the whole thing hasn't imploded."

"Sister!" Zerachu hisses.

"What?" Beatrix says. "It's true."

"Okay, so this time-travel spell," I say. "How far back are we going?"

It sounds weird coming out of my mouth. I mean, I've heard of time travel, don't get me wrong. And scientifically speaking, it's plausible in a fucked-up sort of way. But never in my existence have I heard of the entire world going back in time.

Then again, if it's ever happened, I wouldn't remember.

"We're going back to the day the first half of the *Book of Origin* was taken from Rachel," Beatrix says, sorting through other ingredients attached to her waist.

Okay, so this does sound pretty cool. But there's one thing I'm dying to know. "So, will we appear where we were a little over a week ago? Or will we be staying right here?"

"We will all remain in position"—she sticks out her palm when she spots me opening my mouth to ask another question—"and before you ask, anything you carried in your possession at the time will be returned to you here."

"So," I start, but it's like Beatrix is reading my mind.

"The Heart of Danu and the *Book of Origin* will be returned to us," she says.

And then something hits me. Veerka. She won't remember any of this. Talk about confusing for her. All she'll know is that Lucius is being accused of treason and that she's being assigned his position. It's probably better this way. At least she won't forget our steamy sex. If we're going back about a week, it should leave those memories intact.

"And I take it this spell won't work with only the two of you?" I ask.

By two of you, I'm referring to the Great Witches.

Beatrix shakes her head. "Three witches!"

"Of the same blood," I mumble. "Yeah, yeah, I get it."

I part my lips, prepared to question them both on the whole bringing people back to life thing, when Zerachu sticks her nose in the air and says, "And before you ask, yes, anyone who passed vill be brought back, including Lucius. It has already been arranged zhat he be sent to Hellfire City zhe moment ve travel back."

Okay, seriously? I'm beginning to think their mind reading abilities extend beyond family.

"And how the hell are you going to explain that to the vampires? To Asmodeus?" I ask.

"Asmodeus has been brought to zhe Elder Court," she says. "And have some faith, Alexis. Sheesh. Zhe council is taking care of zhe logistics."

Now that's a weird image. I can't picture Asmodeus setting foot inside the Court. What did he do? Wait until nightfall? And how creepy must that have been? A super ancient vampire walking across a moonlit field to join the Elders.

Weird.

I watch in silence as Beatrix concocts some weird potion made of fine herbs, pink dust, and a thick gooey liquid that looks like bug guts.

"Step back," she orders, and everyone but Zerachu and Rachel moves away.

"Wait!" Rachel says. She rushes next to the motel bed, picks up the iguana—the same lizard I found myself being swallowed by when it was a dragon—and places him into Riskus's arms. She lets out a forced chuckle. "Wouldn't want him becoming a dragon again."

"You think?" I say through gritted teeth.

She rejoins her great-aunts at the center of the destroyed motel room and beams like she's about to receive a Christmas gift. I get it. The kid's about to perform a spell even more experienced witches wish they could attempt.

It's a huge deal.

"*Gambar alleyafus*," Beatrix says.

"Gambar alleyafus," the others repeat.

Beatrix pours the vile of cloudy liquid on the floor in front of them. It bubbles fiercely and a thick cloud of smoke sweeps through the air and into the starlit sky overhead.

"*Astrad nooyar*," Beatrix says.

Again, the others repeat.

She continues to speak gibberish only to be repeated each time until finally, the three of them chant something that sends shivers down my back.

"*Trusdan, tempus itenramus.*"

"Trusdan, tempus itenramus."

"Trusdan, tempus itenramus."

A bright green glow lights up their faces as they lock hands and chant with hunched postures.

I glance sideways at Drax and Ace. They appear as entranced as I am.

They repeat the phrase one more time, but this time, their voices merge into one deep, hollow voice that fills up the entire room.

"Trusdan, tempus itenramus."

Suddenly, a white light flashes so brightly that everything disappears. I blink hard, my surroundings slowly coming back into view.

Mr. Mushroom barks and the whole gang looks at him. On the bed are all sorts of items—a sword, a few knives, a lot of potions, my freaking weapons belt with my Glocks, and on the very corner is the Heart of Danu resting atop the *Book of Origin*. And not merely half the book, but the entire book.

Oh, thank the goddesses.

Well, I suppose I should be thanking the Great Witches—and, of course, Rachel.

"The book!" Rachel says, rushing to the bed.

"My potions!" exclaims Beatrix.

Zerachu is the next one to rush to the bed, her wiry hair dancing atop her head. "My brass knuckles!"

Ace and I glance at each other, and I can't help but smile. Zerachu's one hell of a nutjob, but it's hard not to love her. The next thing I notice is the ceiling—it's back.

This is way too fucking weird.

"It worked," I say.

Zerachu pulls at her long peppermint-green cloak and rushes to the curtained window to peek outside. "Yes, it vould appear it has. Ve did it."

Rachel pumps a skinny fist in the air.

Grinning from ear to ear, she glances sideways at me like she's waiting for praise. Ah, hell. She deserves it.

I pat her on the head. "You did good, kid."

Her excited grin transforms into a sweet smile,

and with a quick shrug, she says, "Thanks. Couldn't have done it without my great-aunts. Or without any of you, really."

I'm about to say, "Okay, okay, we get it. What do you want? An award?" but I swallow my words.

This is her moment, and she deserves to soak it all in. I move toward her and wrap an arm around her shoulders. She winces and tries to pull away, but I hold on and squeeze tight. "I'm proud of you."

"Um, thanks," she says, slipping out of my grasp.

It doesn't offend me. If anything, it makes me smile—she reminds me of me. I can tell she enjoyed the hug, but she'll never admit it.

"So, what's next?" I ask.

Crossing his arms, Ace lets out a sigh of relief. "Well, that's up to you to decide."

I peek down at his manhood and offer a mischievous smirk.

"That's a given," he says.

Rachel smacks my shoulder and gives me the *Ew, get a room* look. "First of all, we should be focusing on what we're gonna do with the *Book of Origin* and the Heart of Danu," she says.

I grab the heart-shaped pendant's chain and raise it to eye level. It sparkles every time it twirls in a circle, and I can't help but be mesmerized by its beauty. The thing might be ravishing, but it's also dangerous in the wrong hands. I want to give it Rachel—I really, really do—but she's still too young, and everyone knows how easy it is for power to go to one's head.

So instead, I turn to Zerachu. "You should be its keeper."

Her sister beams, wraps an arm around her twin, and kisses her cheek. "I couldn't agree more, sis."

"Are you sure?" Zerachu asks. "Zhis is a big deal."

"I'm sure," I say. "It belonged to your sister, and one day it will belong to Rachel."

The sweet expression on Zerachu's face reverts to her usual scowl. "Are you calling me old?"

Before I can answer, she belts out a laugh so loud the vibrations tickle the tip of my nose.

"And what about the book?" I ask. "You got anywhere safe for that?"

"I do," Zerachu says.

Of course she does. She's the Great Witch. She probably has an entire chamber full of crazy shit that no shadow dweller can locate.

"But," she continues, "I don't zhink anyone should have both zhe Heart of Danu and zhe book."

"You want me to guard it?" I ask. "I have a chest in my apartment—"

Everyone's eyes get so big that I stop talking.

"Okay, bad idea," I say.

Slowly, our focus shifts to Beatrix, who stands awkwardly like she's about to be asked to give a classroom presentation. She jabs a finger into her chest and says, "Me?"

Considering she sided with Jamieson less than twenty-four hours ago, I can see why she'd be reluctant to believe we'd trust her with anything of this magnitude. But it's fair to say that Beatrix has proven herself time and time again. And besides, Jamieson doesn't control her anymore. She may have thought that he'd stolen her soul, but he was full of shit. All he did was brainwash her into believing that.

"It makes sense," I say. "You're capable of handling it, and you can keep it somewhere far away from the Heart of Danu."

The two witches stare at each other, making faces as they communicate telepathically, until finally, Zerachu says, "Okay, zis is zhe plan."

"Good," I say. "Glad that's out of the way. And what about you, kid? You gonna go back home to your mom and live out a normal teenager's life?"

Her gaze slowly shifts to her great-aunts, her features hardening deviously.

"What's going on?" I ask.

She balloons her cheeks. It's like she's trying to keep all the words from exploding out of her mouth. When the pressure's too high, she lets out a loud breath and says, "I'm going to Silverstone Witching Academy!"

My eyes bulge out so far something strains. Silverstone? That place is the most advanced witch school in the world. It's prestigious, and it better be at the price they charge—fifty thousand dollars per semester. Then again, that was five years ago. It's probably even more expensive now.

How is this even possible? I'm about to interrogate her on it when I catch a hint of a smile flash across Zerachu's face.

Holy shit. She's orchestrating all of this, and with good reason. Rachel has so much potential. It makes sense that her great-aunt would want her to succeed as a witch.

"Isn't that a four-year program?" I ask.

"Six," Zerachu cuts in. "Finest school in zhis dimension."

"Yeah, I know," I say, my jaw hanging slack.

Rachel is beyond excited, making it impossible not to mimic her expression.

"Holy shit, kid. This is huge."

She balls two fists and wiggles them on either side of her beet-red face. "Right!"

Six years. I'm super stoked for her, but I didn't imagine I'd have to go six years without seeing her. That's how Silverstone works and everyone knows it. Students live at the academy and aren't allowed any external influences for the entire duration of their studies.

It's serious stuff. Half of the students sent to Silverstone are sent back home within their first year because they don't have what it takes. The other half continue into the second year, and from there, another half drop from the program. Those who make it to the sixth year go on to lead extremely successful lives. Most of them are assigned positions within the Elder Court.

Have I mentioned how huge this is? Well, again, this is fucking huge.

Before letting my emotional awkwardness get the best of me, I hug her hard and say, "You might be a little shit, but I am going to miss you."

She doesn't pull away this time. Instead, she digs her face into my neck and I squeeze her even tighter. My throat swells, but I refuse to let a single tear be juiced out of my eyeballs. Finally, I grab her by the shoulders, position her at arm's length, and say, "You're one hell of a witch, you know that?"

She smirks the way I do when someone tells me I'm hot, and says, "I know."

It's arrogance so subtle and playful that it can't even be misinterpreted as cocky.

"I get that you can't leave campus once you're there," I say, "but I hope you'll at least come to visit me when it's over."

She gives me a one-shoulder shrug. "Maybe."
Little shithead.
Then she adds, "Where will I find you?" She shakes her head as if trying to erase her question. "I mean, I'll know how to find you with a location spell, but where will you be? Six years. That's a long time. You got any plans?"

I aim my gaze at Drax, and then Ace. "With friends."

Zerachu gives me the stink-eye. "And vat am I?

Chop liver?"

Beatrix leans in. "The saying is *chopped*, sister."

Zerachu's nose crinkles, pulling her lip over her upper teeth. "Vat?"

Beatrix waves a hand and shakes her head. "Never mind."

"You aren't chopped liver," I say, reaching for Zerachu's shoulder. "Seriously. I can't thank you enough for everything you've done."

Her cold features don't soften, but I can tell she appreciates the words.

"And besides, aren't you going back to the Dark Hall?" I ask.

Out of nowhere, Beatrix punches the air and I flinch. "Oh, please say yes, sister! I've always wanted to work there!"

Zerachu's disgusted look shifts over to her sister. "And vat? Steal my gig?"

"Of course not," Beatrix says. "I have my talents too, you know."

"Like vat?" Zerachu says. "Going evil?"

Beatrix smacks her sister upside the head and Rachel bursts out laughing.

"I'm sure you two can figure something out," I say. "To answer your question, Rachel, I'm planning on changing careers."

Everyone's jaw drops.

"I know, I know. I'm pretty awesome at killing. But I don't know. I think it's time for me to move onto something a little less, mortal, fatal, lethal..."

"Like vat?" Zerachu says.

I shrug. "Not sure yet. Maybe private investigations. Or, maybe a bounty hunter. That'd be pretty sick, too. It's basically what I do now, minus the kill."

Rachel stiffens her posture and beams. "I'm proud of you, Alexis."

I stick my palm up before she can say anything more. "It's not a sure thing, kid, so don't get your hopes up. Maybe I'll miss killing too much. I get one hell of a feed from it."

As the words come out, I can't help but shift my focus onto Ace. Speaking of hungry.

Zerachu throws her arms into the air. "All right, all right! I cannot take zhis sexual energy any longer. Come on, everyone. Let's leave zhe two lovebirds alone."

She heads for the door, Mr. Mushroom and Riskus rushing to her side, and guides everyone out of the motel room, leaving Ace and me alone.

He smiles, and I can't help but stare at his plush pink lips, his thick brown eyebrows, his five-o'clock shadow...

"If this is what you want to do, can I join you?" he asks.

I grab his leather jacket and pull him to me, smelling his crisp deodorant with a hint of dirt. "You need a shower," I say.

He rubs something off the tip of my nose. "So do you."

I'm about to kiss him when I realize I need to clarify something.

"You do understand we can never be exclusive, right?"

"What do you mean?" he asks.

"We can never belong to each other, Ace. We're both incubi demons. I can't feed off you without robbing you of your energy, and vice versa."

Slowly, he reaches for a strand of hair dangling over my cheek and brushes it behind my ear. "I understand, Alexis, so I have a proposition. I feed and share my energy with you."

Is he fucking kidding me?

I smack him hard on the chest and he bursts out laughing—the most gratifying sound I've heard in a long time. Well, aside from the sounds he makes when I'm pleasuring him.

"It was a joke, Alexis. Despite what you might think, I do have a sense of humor."

"Could'a fooled me," I say.

Still touching my face, he leans in to kiss my forehead. "We can't change what we are. As long as I get to enjoy this"—he pushes me back to give me a full up-and-down—"goddess of a body."

"Demi," I say, and he laughs again.

I could get used to that sound.

"All I'm saying," he continues, "is that I am fully on board with whatever type of nonmonogamous relationship you want to have."

I flick his bottom lip and kiss him hard. With my

lips now grazing his, I say, "I'm glad we're on the same page."

"Well, mostly," he says.

I pull my head back to look at him.

"Here you are discussing our relationship status, when all I can think about is dragging you into the shower and having my way with you."

I part my lips to argue, but I can't. The guy's right.

"Well, what the hell are you waiting for?" I say. "Don't just stand there. Shut me up and get me inside that shower."

He bows his head, shadows accentuating his beauty. "As you wish, my goddess."

Now that's more like it.

He scoops me up into his strong arms, and I hold my head against his, breathing him in.

Sex, power, awesome friends. What more could a girl want? I get the feeling I'm about to start a whole new chapter in this crazy life of mine.

Visit **www.shadeowens.com** for more works by Shade Owens.

www.ingramcontent.com/pod-product-compliance
Lightning Source LLC
Chambersburg PA
CBHW030925210726
48290CB00007B/2071